OWL IN DUE CURSE

OWL STAR WITCH MYSTERIES BOOK 10

LEANNE LEEDS

Owl in Due Curse
ISBN: 978-1-950505-74-6
Published by Badchen Publishing
14125 W State Highway 29
Suite B-203 119
Liberty Hill, TX 78642 USA

For permissions contact: info@badchenpublishing.com

CONTENTS

OWL IN DUE CURSE

CHAPTER ONE

"*Ayla*, that gaudy wreath isn't even with the rest of them!" Aunt Gwennie called to my sister, who was slow to react. She shielded her eyes from the light streaming in from the window as she looked up at the wreath our aunt was pointing to.

The adolescent turned and glared at our aunt. "Which wreath? Honoring who?" Ayla pointed to the dozens of wreaths that hung like crown molding around the room. "I've just hung thirty-seven of them in this room, and half of 'em are a little gaudy. You'll have to be more specific than that."

The scent of hydrangea and dahlia from many of the god-honoring wreaths hanging above our heads pervaded the room. Mom decided—without consultation with any of us—to honor the Olympic gods with wreaths at our holiday party. She then randomly added additional honorifics for minor deities to ensure the room was fully encircled with the leafy decorations.

"That wreath with the goat on it." Aunt Gwennie waved toward the circle with a little golden goat hung askew at the edge of the room. "Who's that supposed to honor?" She squinted. "I can't tell from here."

The wreath in question was a masterpiece. Each white and purple pansy, dahlia, and laughing willow leaf had been delicately woven with painstaking detail, finished with a spray of gold paint the color of the cheerful goat gleaming in the candlelight. "Pan, Aunt Gwennie," my sister Althea told her as she walked in and placed a plate of figs on the table next to Ayla. "Honoring the goat-footed demigod Pan."

"One of the god-honoring wreaths is for Pan? Pan?" Aunt Gwennie's face scrunched. "Did you tell your mother you were honoring Pan?" No one answered, and she continued. "Now, girls, you know I'm a strict follower of Athena. I would never insult one of the gods, demigods, or otherwise—but I have to ask you. Is Pan really the energy we want to call to a house with all women during the holidays?" Aunt Gwennie put her palms on her ample hips and looked around at the eclectic mix of wreaths. "That doesn't seem appropriate. Not at all."

"Pan, the god of shepherds and flocks," my sister Ami reminded our aunt as she sat down and removed her new straw hat. "Nothing wrong with that, Aunt Gwennie."

"The god of shepherds and flocks? You think that's what everyone remembers about that old goat?" Aunt Gwennie waved a hand dismissively, dismissing the Ami's words. "Yes, I'm sure that's the energy Althea intended. Because she's so fond of farm animals."

"Aunt Gwennie!" Althea gasped.

"Actually, I like Pan's deeper lessons." My sister Ayla grabbed a cube off a plate of cheese and grapes with a flourish. "The god of shepherds and flocks. Oh, and the god of rustic music. He's super well-rounded."

"That horn-dog shepherd is a thing we shouldn't talk about in polite conversation, and you girls know it," Aunt Gwennie scoffed. "I just don't think it's a proper honorific for a Christmas party."

"Brumalia. Let's use the Hellenic term, please,"

my mother corrected as she floated in to the room dressed in a stunning holiday dress. A long, gauzy purple skirt billowed around her ankles while a white top with wide bell sleeves hung elegantly off her shoulders and down to her hips.

"Brumalia is Roman, Mother," I told her wryly.

"Roman gods are borrowed from Greek mythology. It's all the same," my mother said with a wave of her hand. "Besides, the invitation said to honor the gods in your own way, and what's more personal than honoring a god personally?"

I blinked. "Wait, what are we talking about now?"

"Althea's wreath for Pan."

"No." Aunt Gwennie shook her head emphatically and put her hands on her hips again. "During the winter solstice, it's all about the Hellenic gods. Athena, Ares, Zeus. Hermes, Demeter, Apollo. And Hermes' son, Dionysus. Not Pan! I just don't like the energy."

"My goodness, don't be such a prude, Gwennie." My mother sat next to Ami, a large golden wreath on her head. "I disagree, Gert. Pan is a very appropriate honorific for a holiday party, especially one hosted by women at the winter solstice. Pan is also the god of male sexuality. You know that. While most of the time I would agree with you that Pan has no place here,"—she glanced at me with an eyebrow raised—"considering how long it's taking Astra to commit to Jason, I can't believe inviting Pan to the party would hurt anything. It may even be useful." Mom reached up and adjusted the wreath on her head.

"Mother!"

She looked up at me innocently. "What? Tell me I'm wrong."

Aunt Gwennie crossed her arms over her chest and pursed her lips. "But Pan is...look, I'm not happy with the choices made by the girls here, and I won't apologize for my opinion."

"Hold on a minute. Girls?" Ami pointed at Aunt Gwennie. "That's Althea's wreath. How did the rest of us get roped into her deity choices? I didn't get a vote, and knowing Thea, I doubt Astra or Ayla did, either."

"Thanks for the support, sis." She smiled sarcastically at Ami and lifted her own glass of non-alcoholic mead in a mock toast. "Aunt Gwennie, you're infringing on my freedom of religion," Althea told our aunt.

"Hmph." Aunt Gwennie crossed her arms and

looked out the big picture window over the backyard. "Damn goat-god."

"Pan is a god that interests me and makes me happy. So I hung his wreath." She shrugged. "I even got water for the punch from Lake Monroe."

Aunt Gwennie looked over at our sister, her gray eyes narrowed. "And how do you honor Pan, Althea? Aren't you a little young to be honoring a god so obscene?"

"Aunt Gwennie!" Althea gasped, outraged and blushing.

"I'm just saying," my aunt held her hands up. "When the horn-dog is supposed to be an inspiration for one to sow their wild oats, the last thing we need is a wreath of his at a family gathering woven together by a seventeen-year-old witch." Aunt Gwennie glanced at me. "Well, maybe your mother's right. We could hang it in your room."

* * *

MY THREE SISTERS and I had worked the last two days to get the house ready for my mother's Brumalia (or winter solstice or Christmas) party. Our house, a large colonial converted farmhouse in Forkbridge, Florida, housed my mother and aunt, my three sisters, and my owl familiar, Archie. Now that we had so many friends and new paranormals in town—the vampires like Emma's brother, Rex, and the werewolves like Emma's boyfriend Eddie...

Yeah, my friend Emma seemed to attract paranormals. A vampire brother, a werewolf boyfriend, a witch best friend—that would be me, by the way.

Anyway.

My mother decided it was important for us to have a party for the local paranormals.

I had to admit our house looked beautiful. I mean, it normally was, with wood floors in the living room, kitchen, and dining room, and parquet in the bathrooms. The walls were white, with peach and green curtains and wall art. It was bright, and airy, with enough space for all of us to feel at ease, regardless of age. There was even a detached garage that had been converted into a new age shop, supplying crystals, herbs, and potions to the magically inclined locals and tourists.

But with the holiday decorations?

The house looked...well, magical.

We had decorated with fake snow, pine, and oak leaves. The living room had a new agey theme centered on the winter solstice, with candles and crystals, and the wreaths crowning the room like it had its own tiara. It was done in red and white, with red pillows on the white sofa and white candles on red candlesticks. The altar placed against one wall had candles and herbs.

Everything smelled divine…but even so, I was happy to have a place to retreat to.

A place where I could be alone.

"You know, they have a point," Archie said, leaning against the wall and staring out the open window of my attic bedroom. His head swiveled and twisted, his eyes meeting mine with an intent stare. "Well, your mother has a point. You've been dating Jason for a long time. Longer than Emma and Eddie have been dating—and I'm sure I don't need to point out that she's pregnant with the werewolf's baby. You two haven't even spent the night together."

"So?" I asked. Archie's comment wasn't unexpected; my mom and my sisters had been asking me about Jason and a wedding ever since we came back from that stupid island camping trip. They worried I was putting off marriage like my mother and Aunt Gwennie—ironic, right?— and even with my mother's long life span as Athena's high priestess, they wanted grandchildren while they were still young enough to move around easily. Apparently, my desire for children depended on their sciatica. "Aunt Gwennie's just having a midlife crisis."

"If you're staying with Jason, you're going to have to commit sooner rather than later, Astra," Archie told me as if the next step in my life was obvious. "You're no spring chicken, you know."

I took a deep breath, ready to pop back a retort. But then I exhaled.

I wasn't a spring chicken, but I wasn't some old maid, either. I was thirty-four years old. The median age at first marriage for women was twenty-eight years in the United States. I wasn't that far behind.

Besides, I didn't want to get married.

I definitely didn't want to have a baby.

Not now.

Not yet.

Not this soon.

"I'm not ready. I've barely adjusted to being out of the military. I like my job at the police department,"—as a psychic consultant partnering with Emma (when she wasn't as big as a house) —"and I'm finally comfortable at home. Like, really comfortable."

"Congratulations," the owl said with a tilt of

his head. "You're a well adjusted teenager. What do you want, a medal?"

"Oh, come on." I glared at him. "The relationship with Jason and me? It's more complicated than all of you are making it out to be. I know you don't understand because you're an owl and divine and all that, but this is a big deal for me. I don't have to get married. There are other options."

"For you and for Jason, yes, but one has to consider others. Jason's put up with you for over a year. Practically since you came back to Forkbridge. You've put him off repeatedly."

"So?" I asked. "What's wrong with that? Maybe he's waiting for me." I shifted uncomfortably. "Isn't that supposed to be romantic or something?"

"Okay, center of the universe—are you waiting for him?" Archie asked in a low, serious tone. "I mean, the only time you spend with Jason is at family events lately. Or double dating with wolves. You two are practically never alone together. At least Emma and Eddie have time together. Wasn't that his biggest complaint when you each had your issues on the truth-telling island thing?"

I sighed. "Why are we even talking about this?"

"What else should we talk about?"

"It's my life, Archie."

"True. It's your life. You're the first child and heir of Arden House. You have responsibilities, right?" Archie arched his head down and preened as I shivered and shuddered at the thought of taking over for my mother as Athena's high priestess. As if he sensed my discomfort, he gave words to my fear. "What if you have to take over for your mother?"

A knock on the attic door blocked my retort. "Come in," I called to whichever sister was at the bottom of the stairs.

The door opened, and Althea poked her head in. "Are you decent?" she called up.

"Yep."

"I thought you might take a nap before the party," my sister said as she raced loudly up the steps. "Aren't you going to change?" She sat down on the end of my bed, her gold and green dress rustling in her movement. "You don't look like you're in your old uniform, but that's not exactly party clothes." She glanced at my white tank top and faded jeans. "Well, not party clothes in this decade. A leather jacket and you'd make a good biker in the fifties."

"I'm going to change in a minute." I jerked my head toward the dress hanging to Althea's right. The fabric was sleek, the color a rich and dark purple that reminded me of plums. A small dark red blazer with white buttons hung on a hook opposite the mirror and sparkled when the light from outside the window hit it. "What do you think?"

She cocked an eyebrow, her smile barely hidden. "It's nice," she said, then she paused and placed a hand on her chin. "You realize it looks like a uniform."

"It does not."

"Your older sister has a very defined comfort zone," Archie told Althea.

"Yeah, speaking of," she said as she shifted forward. "I wanted to apologize about the wreath thing downstairs." Thea, now seventeen, was the second to youngest sister—even though she was so stoic and serious you'd think she was far older than she was. "It didn't even occur to me Aunt Gwennie would be so annoyed about my wreath, or that it would somehow involve your dating life."

I started to interrupt and tell her it was okay, but she held up a hand and continued.

"Yes, I know what you're going to say. I should have thought of that when I made that wreath—"

"I was not going to say that," I sighed as I picked up the red suit jacket and turned to face the mirror. My reflection stared back at me as I held up the jacket and examined myself, all primped and ready for my mother's party. My lips were a dark plum, and I wore my hair in a twist, with a few strands falling around my neck. "It has nothing to do with me or Jason, Thea, which god you honor at the party."

"Don't get me wrong. I like Jason," Thea continued, as if she didn't hear me. "He's a good guy. Good looking. Caring. Supportive."

I stared at her.

She stared back.

"What?" I demanded.

She shrugged, her face the picture of innocence. "I was just thinking. Maybe you don't have to be so passionate about Jason. You know? Maybe it's enough that he's a good guy and you have fun with him."

I stared some more.

She shrugged. "Okay, I'm going to go finish getting ready. People will start arriving soon."

* * *

I RETURNED to the mirror and stared at myself for a long time. I wasn't sure where she got it, but Thea's off-the-cuff remark was more accurate than she realized: I felt little passion for Jason.

I cared about him. He was a great friend.

The relationship was…comfortable.

But comfortable wasn't something you started with.

Was it?

I wondered why I didn't feel more passionate about Jason. He was good looking, and he could be sweet when he wanted to be. But there was always something holding me back from fully committing to him. Falling for Jason was easy, but my reservations about the relationship…

I sighed and shook my head, trying to clear my thoughts. It wasn't the time or place for this, I told myself firmly. I could rationalize anything when it suited me. I needed to focus on the party.

I quickly finished getting ready, slipping into the dark purple dress and pulling on the suit jacket over it. As I stood in front of the mirror once more, looking at my reflection with a mixture of wonder and anxiety, I wondered what was really bothering me.

I sighed once more and pushed wispy hair from my eyes, suddenly feeling overwhelmed by a torrent of questions. Was there something bothering me? Something clouding my thoughts and preventing me from truly connecting with Jason?

As the minutes passed, I felt a flicker of unease grow inside me.

Was this the first sign that our relationship was headed for trouble?

"The first sign?" Archie asked, his beak letting out an oddly owlish snort as he jumped on my shoulder. "The writing's been on the wall for weeks, months even," he said matter-of-factly, his golden eyes fixed on mine in the mirror. "You can't keep living in denial, Astra. Eventually you're going to have to deal with this issue."

I frowned at him. "Stay out of my head."

"No."

"And just what issue is that?" I asked skeptically. I couldn't believe there was anything that Archie could see that I couldn't.

I was in the darn relationship.

He was an owl.

Archie fixed me with a level stare. "You humans are so obtuse sometimes. It's like you can see the issue right in front of your face, but you refuse to acknowledge it."

I frowned at him. "What are you talking about?"

The owl hooted softly and flapped his wings in an agitated manner. "Thea was right, you know," he said. "You don't feel passion for Jason because he doesn't truly ignite any spark within you. You don't feel that fire burning inside of you when you're with him. And I think you know it, too."

I shook my head, not wanting to believe what Archie was saying—and a little annoyed that everyone passed judgment on my relationship the night of the Christmas—um, Solstice party.

But as I descended the stairs as the doorbell ran, I feared deep down he was right.

CHAPTER TWO

The colorful lights strung throughout the house and across the porch swayed slightly in the warm December wind. In most places, the night warmth of August was already traded for the brisk chill of winter.

But not here in Central Florida. The temperature rarely fell below sixty.

The house smelled like fresh pine needles and sugar cookies, and I could hear faint echoes of Bob Marley's 'One Love' playing from somewhere inside.

I looked around, taking in the flurry of activity around me. Guests drifted in and out of the rooms as groups of people endlessly migrated from food to music to outside to the couch. I watched quietly as they flowed, almost like blood recirculating through an artery.

The werewolves laughed and flirted on the patio with the mayor of Cassandra (and Jason's mother) as the chief looked on, and groups of pixies huddled together inside ooh-ing and aah-ing over the snacks as Serena Bliss (Jason's ex-girlfriend) explained what crab puffs were. Everyone was dressed to the nines, their outfits gleaming beneath the twinkling lights strung across the ceiling.

I drew my gaze to Jason, who was chatting with my best friend Emma and her boyfriend—and baby daddy—Eddie Renzo near the bar. He looked as handsome and confident as he usually did, his half-smile and dimples flashing as he laughed boisterously at whatever story they were sharing.

As I looked around, I couldn't help noticing that everyone was smiling, except me. I glanced down at my drink. A seasonal-themed cocktail sat lifeless in my hand. I watched as the ice cubes tumbled around in their red fluid prison.

What if Archie was right?

What if I didn't feel passion for Jason because he ignited no spark within me?

What did that mean?

I had been dating Jason for over a year now, and in that time, he had shown himself to be a caring and thoughtful man. He put my happiness before everything else, and I felt appreciated more than I had ever been in my life. He was everything a wonderful boyfriend should be.

But…was that enough?

It should be, I told myself as I sipped my drink. I knew women that would celebrate a strong man with a gentle heart and good sense of humor who treated them well. So he didn't make my heart race.

So what?

I loved being around Jason. He made me feel safe and secure, and I liked the life we had together. That had to be enough, right?

"You look like you have the weight of the world on your shoulders." I turned to find Lothian Pennington, a werewolf, standing next to me, a drink in hand. He was watching me intently, his expression one of concern.

"I'm fine," I told him and turned away.

As much as I hated to admit it—and I couldn't stand him, so I really didn't want to—Lothian Pennington was one of the most attractive men I'd ever seen.

"Are you?"

I turned to glare at him.

Lothian was tall with broad shoulders and a muscular build. His slightly wavy dark hair had a silver streak that seemed to have always been there, and it weirdly brought out the intensity of his piercing blue eyes. He wore a black button-down shirt that hugged his chest perfectly and black dress pants that sat low on his hips.

I mean, the man looks like he stepped out of a GQ magazine.

"I said I'm fine," I lied, giving him a tight smile.

Lothian didn't look convinced, but he didn't press the issue. "This is quite the party," he said, his eyes scanning the room as he turned his attention to the surrounding party. "You ladies have truly outdone yourselves."

"Yup," I answered sharply, hoping the sting in my tone would get across to the werewolf that I thought he was a pompous ass and I had no interest in talking to him.

We had a conflict on Owl Key a few months ago, and even though he was a member of Eddie Renzo's wolf pack, I still didn't trust him. (That was especially true now that he was the owner of Owl Key after a time travel snafu actually more like a conspiracy on his part to snatch the private island.)

A manipulator was something I couldn't stand.

Unfortunately, Lothian didn't seem deterred by my icy demeanor.

Instead, he pulled me into an intense stare, a look that was more than a mere feeling. It seemed something tangible that I could almost reach out and touch. His eyes glittered with amusement, and I suddenly could not look away. "What?" I snapped.

"You look lovely tonight," he chuckled softly, his voice low. "I grew concerned that you were over here all alone looking glum, that's all. A woman like you should be flirted with at a party, not ignored." Lothian grinned then, giving me a wink as he moved even closer. "I took it upon myself to rectify the error."

I put down my drink, put my hands on my hips and glared at him defiantly, refusing to let him rattle me with his flirtation. "Don't flatter yourself," I said coldly, cutting him down in a sharp tone. "I'm not interested in you or your ridiculous sweet-talking tactics. I have no interest in being toyed with by some arrogant alpha-wannabe like you. You're a dime a dozen."

"Am I?" He stepped even closer so close we were standing mere inches apart.

I stepped back, putting at least two feet between us. The nerve of this guy! "Yes. Now back off. Again—I'm not interested in your meaningless flattery."

Lothian laughed, unaffected by my rejection. "If you change your mind, you know where to find me," he said with a wink before sauntering off toward Eddie and Emma—and Jason—with a smirk on his lips.

"Overconfident jerk," I muttered as I watched him go, gritting my teeth in frustration.

Lothian Pennington was the last person I wanted to talk to, let alone flirt with. He was an arrogant, self-centered jerk who thought he was the gods' gift to women. He walked around with a swagger, like he owned the world.

"Self-absorbed narcissist," I added under my breath.

The party continued around me, but I was no longer in the mood to socialize. Lothian's presence had put a damper on my evening.

* * *

I TRIED to push Lothian out of my mind as I mingled with the other guests, but it was difficult. He seemed to be everywhere I turned, his tall frame and striking features making him impossible to miss.

I stormed away from the party and out onto the terrace, furious. Why did I let him get to me? Lothian would be here as part of our circle until he left Eddie's wolf pack—if that would happen, anyway. I had no say over the werewolves, not as a witch and not as Athena's little star card wind-up witch. One way or another, I'd have to figure out how to deal with him. Especially once Emma had her baby.

"How come he bothers you so much?" Archie asked, precariously balanced on the wrought-iron fence, his talons full of beef jerky sticks. He ripped into one as he waited for my response.

"I don't know. I just don't like him." The night air was cool as it washed over me, but it did nothing to calm my raging emotions and towering resentments. I needed a moment alone to clear my head. "He actually tried to flirt with me."

"Not for nothing, but that doesn't exactly make you special," Archie responded. "He made your Aunt Gwennie blush. I swear, that man thinks the sun comes up just to hear him crow."

As I stood there gazing at the town of Forkbridge, barely visible through the trees, a bolt of lightning split the skies above me. The wind rushed against my skin as I squinted at the churning clouds above. A crackle of thunder reverberated through the air, and then suddenly, everything went still once again.

"What on Earth was that?" I asked Archie, who was staring blankly at the horizon.

Suddenly, there was a loud ringing at the door.

Archie tilted his head to the side, as if he was trying to listen to something. He paused for a few moments before finally saying, "Somebody's at the door," in a low voice. Then he tore at the beef jerky.

"No. You think?" I said as I rolled my eyes. "I'll get it," I said with finality as I sighed and turned around.

As I stepped into the room, I could hear a faint voice coming from the other side, almost like someone was shouting through a tin can. Intrigued, I clutched the door handle and pulled it open…

…only to find a toy soldier…or a knight…or a prince, maybe…standing at attention.

"Unexpected," I muttered, staring.

It was a beautiful carving, with intricate details and a glossy finish. The soldier was standing at attention and a small owl was carved like a logo on his right breast. It was white, almost like marble, and it seemed to glow with an otherworldly sparkle.

I picked up the soldier and examined it, turning it over in my hands. I nearly dropped it when he opened his mouth and announced that he was here to see Archimedes the Owl.

"Super unexpected," I said.

"I rang the doorbell," he responded tartly.

"Who are you?" I asked. "And why do you want to see Archie?"

The figure smiled at me and nodded his head. "I can't tell you my name or where I'm from," he said calmly. "But I have a message for Archie from our queen."

"Your queen? Queen who?" I responded, determined to get something concrete out of this enchanted Christmas toy. After all, the last time a gift showed up on the Ardens' doorstep, I got linked to a divine owl, a goddess I didn't believe in, and a job that doesn't pay at all.

The soldier stared up at me silently, his chiseled features perfectly stoic. But...there was something about his eyes that seemed to burn with a sense of duty and determination. "Archimedes. Please, Ms. Arden."

I felt an uneasy sense of dread settle over me.

"Who's at the door?" Ami asked as she arrived, followed by Althea and Ayla.

I held up the toy soldier.

Her eyes widened at the sight of the sparkling toy.

He waved his small stone arm at Ami. "Ma'am."

"Whoa. What is that?" Ami asked, her voice laced with curiosity.

"This is a toy soldier, I think," I said. "He says he has a message for Archie from some queen."

"That's so weird," Ayla said, coming to inspect.

"So, what's the message for Archie?" Althea asked.

The toy soldier stopped waving and frowned. "I'm sorry, but I can't tell you that," he said. "It's classified. I need to tell Archimedes directly."

Ami arched an eyebrow. "Did you say a queen told you to come here?"

The toy soldier nodded his head.

Just then, Archie came flying into the foyer, his eyes wide and excited. "When you're done with whatever's just arrived at the party, I need one of you to—" He stopped short when he saw the toy soldier in my hands. "No way. It's only been a year!"

"Archie, do you know what this is?" Ami asked Archie in a hushed tone.

"No." Archie repeated. I couldn't tell if he was answering Ami or responding to the toy.

The soldier bowed his head slightly. "I'm afraid so, Archimedes," he breathed. He glanced at me before turning his gaze back to Archie. "Athena wants to ensure that you, Archimedes, are adequately developing into your role as Astra's familiar and the star card guide."

I felt another sense of unease wash over me. Whatever Athena wanted, it couldn't be good. And I knew enough about mythology that failing a test given by a god?

That also couldn't be good.

Archie landed on my other arm, facing the toy soldier. Archie looked at the soldier with a sharp, purposeful eye. He puffed up his chest and stood as straight as an owl perched on a witch's arm could. Archie sighed and flew back down to the floor after a few moments. "It looks real. I mean, I've heard of these things. It happens. It's not supposed to happen after a year. More like a century. But it can happen." The owl looked resigned.

"What happens?" I asked. "What are you talking about?"

"Athena is the goddess of wisdom and strategy," the soldier said slowly. "And she believes that you"—he pointed at Archie—"are not yet ready to fully fulfill your role as a celestial being. But you may be, so she is testing you, challenging you to prove your worth and mastery."

There was an uneasy silence as Ami, Althea, and Ayla stared at the toy.

"What kind of test?" Althea asked hesitantly. "Is it dangerous?"

"Well, I should say tests. It's not just one," the soldier replied grimly. "Obviously it's dangerous. We know Athena for her harsh and merciless ways of testing those who cross her."

"How do I even know if I pass or fail?" Archie demanded.

"That's why I am here. I will tell you. Or you will know because you live or die."

Die?

"What do you mean, die?" I asked him.

A murmur of unease rippled through the group. My three sisters stared at each other anxiously, their eyes full of worry and fear.

"This is ridiculous," Althea exclaimed. "We will not let you threaten our owl."

"Is he really yours, Ms. Arden?" the soldier responded.

"Hey, mouth, are you flammable?" Althea asked angrily, her eyes flashing. "We can end this whole thing right now."

"Are you serious? Your whole shtick makes little sense," Ayla exclaimed, staring at the soldier. "The goddess who sent him here just a year ago wants to put Archie to the test to see if he can stay?" When the soldier nodded, Ayla snapped, "She doesn't have much confidence in her own choices, does she? What kind of garbage is that?"

"No way," Althea said, shaking her head. "I'm telling you, this is a trick. That can't be right."

Ami frowned as she studied the toy soldier closely. "Let's all take a breath and think this through. I agree, there must be more to it than just this," she said, tapping her finger against her chin thoughtfully. "What's the actual message here?"

"Ami," Althea gasped, pointing to Ami's pocket. "Look. Your pocket. It's glowing."

My sister pulled out her tarot deck and stared at it, her face illuminated by the glow. She picked up the top card on the deck and held it up in front of her. It twirled like the hands of a clock before flying out of her hand and into the air toward Archie.

* * *

"THAT MAKES NO SENSE," Lothian said with a confused look on his face.

We huddled in an alcove off the living room, everyone gathered together. The werewolf pack was anxious, while my mother and aunt looked shocked. Ami gripped the star card, her fingers nearly crushing the glossy, glowing surface.

"Of course it does," Althea disagreed. "Archie's life is in danger, and we need to help him. That toy must be a trick."

"What if it's not?" I asked.

"If it's not, then Archie's life is threatened by Athena," Wyatt Marlow, one werewolf, pointed out. "So, the goddess is both threatening his life, and wants you to save him from the same threat?" He frowned. "Lothian's right. That's illogical."

"You haven't read many of the Greek myths, have you?" Jason asked him. "Illogical is a feature in a lot of the stories."

"Hogwash," my mother told him. "Athena is the most levelheaded of all the gods."

"I'm sure both Arachne and Medusa would

disagree with you on that point," Lothian told her.

"Fake news," Aunt Gwennie said with a huff.

"Look, I know I'm just a lowly human here, but we need to focus on helping Archie first," Emma said, looking around the group anxiously, her hand distractedly patting her enormous belly. "You don't work the case first and protect the target later. Protecting Archie comes first." Emma looked at me. "Someone needs to interrogate that toy." Then she wiggled her fingers at me. "You held it. What did you sense?"

I held up my hands. "My gloves."

There was a collective murmur of agreement, and the group made their way over to the soldier. I lingered behind with Archie and watched my sisters march forward with grim determination.

"If that's what you want." The toy soldier remained stoic and unaffected as they crowded around him, shrugging it off as if none of this mattered. "Try to be reasonable here, guys," the soldier said calmly. "Athena has given Archie a rare opportunity to prove himself worthy. Do you really want to take that away from him?"

"What do you mean, prove himself worthy?" Althea demanded. "Prove himself worthy of what?"

The soldier let out a long sigh, as if he was trying to find the patience to deal with us. "Archie is being given the chance to become even better than he is, almost like a god," he explained. "All he has to do is complete a series of tasks for Athena and prove himself. That's it. If he succeeds, we will reward him with immortality."

"I'm already immortal," Archie told the toy soldier.

"Well, a better immortality. Better powers."

Aunt Gwennie snorted in disbelief. "And if he fails?"

The soldier hesitated for a moment, as if he was debating whether to tell us. "If Archie fails," he finally said, his voice low and grave, "we will condemn him to Tartarus, and Astra will get another familiar."

CHAPTER THREE

My mother and Aunt Gwennie, my sisters, and three werewolves in human form. Eddie Renzo, his girlfriend Emma, and my boyfriend, Jason. Through interest and overhearing, this assemblage converged into the group determined to save Archie. The mood as I processed what the toy soldier had told me was somber.

"Merry Christmas?" Emma said with a sarcastic edge to her voice.

The group was silent as we processed the new information, each one of us lost in our own head. "I feel like the holidays around you and this owl are complicated as a rule," Eddie said with a half-smile. "It was pretty weird last year, too."

I didn't smile back.

If Archie failed, he would be sent to Tartarus, the Greek underworld where the worst of criminals were punished. It was a fate worse than death, at least if the myths were to be believed—and there was no coming back from it. At the academy, we were told the souls of those sent there are chained to the ground by their wrists and ankles, with their heads dangling into the river. They remain eternally thirsty, but can never quench that thirst. Or so I'd heard.

"Could you stop thinking about it?" Archie squawked at me.

"Sorry." I nodded, remembering the longer Archie, and I knew one another, the more he seemed to see within my head. I didn't know for sure that he could read my mind, but I'd never asked. "You know, the longer I have this star power, the more these stupid myths are invading my life," I said to no one in particular.

Aunt Gwennie patted my arm sympathetically. "It's not your fault, dear. You didn't ask for any of this." She then reached out and scratched the devastated Archie on the back of the neck. The owl barely raised his eyes in response. "We'll figure it out, Archie."

"Astra, I know you were being kind of

flippant, but you're not wrong," Lothian said, coming to stand next to me. "The longer you have the power, the more you become a part of the mythology. It's inevitable." He glanced at my mother and Aunt Gwennie. "The best option would be to have your mother try to contact Athena. She's Athena's high priestess, after all."

Aunt Gwennie looked around at the group assembled before speaking. When no one disagreed, she said, "It sounds like we're all in agreement then. Minerva?"

My mother appeared dazed. Her expression was blank and her eyes wide. She looked like she didn't know what to say or even where to begin. She mumbled something incoherent and unintelligible in response, her voice nothing more than a crackling whisper.

Aunt Gwennie placed a supportive arm around her. "Minerva's busy at the moment. Anyone have a different plan?"

Althea looked at her with concern. "What's wrong with Mom?"

Aunt Gwennie shook her head.

"I think we need to find out more about these tasks Athena has set for Archie." Jason said as he came to stand on the opposite side of me from the werewolf. I stood sandwiched between the two as if they were the angel/devil dating game sprung to life. "Maybe if we know what they are, we can help him prepare for them."

"Yes, let's follow the human's suggestion," Lothian muttered with an eye roll.

"Sorry?" Jason looked confused. "I just think—"

"What's your problem?" I spat at Lothian, my voice dripping with annoyance.

Lothian opened his mouth to speak as Ami placed a hand on my arm.

"Lothian," Eddie said sharply. "Astra's worried about her familiar. Maybe you should be careful where you step at the moment."

Lothian let out an exasperated sigh and shook his head. "Apologies."

There was a sense of tension, a feeling of urgency in the group—one that seemed at odds with the party continuing on the other side of the closed door as if nothing crazy was happening in the alcove. The clinking of glasses and plates mingled with the laugher of drunken paranormals as they celebrated. It was an odd soundtrack to our concerns.

"I never should have thrown this party," my mother whispered.

"This isn't your fault, either, Minerva," Aunt Gwennie told her.

"Okay, before everyone gets depressed and starts blaming themselves for whatever is going on, Aunt Gertie says there are no unexpected ghosts or spirits around the house," Ayla said.

"Who's Aunt Gertie?" Wyatt Marlow, a quiet werewolf, asked.

"My aunt."

"Ayla is a death speaker," Althea explained.

Since Ayla and my mother were the only two witches that could speak to the dead (and my mother was often busy) it usually fell to Ayla to channel info from beyond.

"I am." Ayla nodded. "She's going to take another trip around the outside again, but other than the talking toy over there, there's nothing. We're still warded and protected."

"My brother's at the party, though. So are the pixies," Emma pointed out. "Didn't you guys have to change your normal wards to let other paranormals in?" She looked at the toy soldier. "I mean, this cursed doll got in, right?"

"Excuse me," the small medieval soldier responded indignantly. "I'm here on a goddess's mission. I do not intend to be mocked by the likes of you. And I am not cursed."

"That entirely depends on which side of this test you sit on, bub," Archie flared back, his voice quavering.

"I sit where I always sit," the soldier responded.

With a look of fierce determination in his eyes, Archie squared his wings and turned to face the toy. "You may think you have all the power here, but I refuse to let you get the best of me," he said, his voice echoing with authority. "I am not some ignorant birdbrain in your stupid game—I am a warrior, a hunter, and a survivor." A wave of energy seemed to flow from him as he spoke, filling him with visible strength and determination. "And I am not alone."

"That's right," Jason said, coming to stand next to Archie. "You're not alone in this, buddy. We're all behind you."

Even Lothian seemed to have softened as he nodded in agreement.

"We will help you, Archie," Aunt Gwennie said with a reassuring smile. "Don't you worry."

The toy soldier's face softened as he faced Archie. "I see now why Athena has chosen you," he said. "You are courageous and brave, two qualities that will be essential in the tasks ahead."

"Hey, yeah, right? So, speaking of—what are

these tasks?" Jason asked casually. "Surely you can tell us what we need to do to help Archie succeed."

"Surely I cannot tell you that," the soldier said. "It is not my place. You'll discover that for yourselves."

"What a surprise," Lothian said, his voice tight with frustration. "Fine. We will find out what we need to know."

"Good luck with that," the toy responded cheerfully.

With a flash of light, the soldier suddenly disappeared into thin air, leaving only the empty pedestal it stood upon in its place. The group stared at the spot where the inanimate yet animated toy had once stood.

"I told you someone should have interrogated him," Emma said in her most judgmental I-told-you-so tone. "But no. You all are so absorbed by your little paranormal world that mere human investigative techniques? Tossed aside." Her index finger jabbed at me, punctuating every other word. Her face was filled with a mix of annoyance and discomfort. "You need to start listening to me."

And then she belched.

* * *

"WE NEED TO BACK UP. What wards did we take down?" Ami asked me as we watched my mother, pale as a sheet, across the alcove. "Emma's right— we let vampires in here, the pixies." She glanced at Eddie. "Obviously, the werewolves. So we must have changed something."

"Not we—just Mom. I'm not sure what she did, but…" I held my hand toward her. "I don't think I've ever seen her so rattled before," I told her. "She mentioned this morning that she was going into meditation to adjust the wards, but she did it alone. I don't know what she did. Did any of you go in with her?"

Everyone shook their heads.

Ami gazed at the walls as if she could see the ancient wards that protected the shell of our home. "To be honest, they don't look tampered with at all, Astra. I mean, not in a bad way." She narrowed her eyes as she looked at the empty pedestal where the cursed toy had been. "But there's no ward that would keep out anything having to do with Athena. Since we're an official Athena temple, she can always get in. Anything connected to her can always get in."

Just then, Althea stepped forward, her gaze

fixed on the empty pedestal. "Why is that still here?" she asked, pointing toward the ground. "That stupid toy boy was all one piece when he was here. He didn't walk. Why'd he leave his hockey puck pedestal behind?" She looked up. "Mom? Do you know anything about this?"

My mother twisted her head to the side with such force that her face contorted, her lips drawn tight with tension.

I turned back to Ami and Althea.

As we all stood there contemplating the next steps and waiting for someone to take charge, a loud crash echoed down the hallway, followed immediately by shrieks and panicked shouts from the party goers.

"What was that?" Lothian asked quickly. When no one answered, he added, "Do you think something else is going on? Or is this test one?"

"How do the gods test people, anyway?" Emma asked. "In your tradition, I mean."

"A spiritual test, according to several religious traditions, is a life situation, provided by one of the gods, to evaluate man's—or owl's—individual moral character," Lothian responded. "So Athena's tests are probably much like your spiritual tests."

Emma chuckled sharply. "Yeah, somehow, I don't think so."

Ayla's eyes shifted between our mom, Althea's face, and the door. "She wouldn't send attackers here, though, would she?" Ayla asked. "I mean, we are still her priestesses."

Althea cleared her throat. "Everyone's putting an awful lot of trust in the words of a Chucky doll. I wouldn't trust that thing to tell the time, let alone tell me the truth about what's going on here."

"She's got a point," Jason said. "What if—"

A pixie burst into the alcove, his face pale and sweaty. "There are monsters in there, and they want our women!" he screamed. "I don't want to die!"

"Lothian, dear, please go check and see what that racket is all about. Take your brothers with you just in case the goddess really manifested some dangerous ruffians," Aunt Gwennie said as she stepped up calmly and took charge of the situation. Her fingers were entwined in the back of my mother's hair, rubbing and caressing it gently.

Lawrence, Norden, and Wyatt followed Lothian out the door.

"Your mother is...unreachable at the

moment," Aunt Gwennie said, her voice calm. A faint glow radiated from her hands as she continued to rub my mother's head.

"What do you mean, unreachable?" Ami asked.

Aunt Gwennie held her hand up. "Now, that could mean a few things. My suspicion is that Minerva's been cut off from communication with Athena because of this little test. That implies Athena really is the one behind whatever Archie is dealing with. Or," she said, tilting her head, "someone is trying to isolate us from Athena."

The earth shook. I looked up at my mother in alarm, but she was staring off into the distance, her face blank.

"What is that?" Althea asked, her voice tight.

"Mom?" I hissed, but she didn't respond. I turned to Ami and Althea. "Do you know what's going on?"

"It feels like an earthquake!" Ami shouted.

"No kidding!" I snapped back.

The shaking intensified, and I grabbed hold of the door frame to keep from being thrown to the ground. Glass shattered and people were screaming. The intricate alcove chandelier crashed to the floor, narrowly missing Aunt Gwennie and my mother.

"We need to get out of here!" Althea yelled.

I saw Althea lose her grip and go sliding across the floor. "Althea!" I shouted, but before I could get to her, the shaking stopped as abruptly as it had started.

Aunt Gwennie was still standing next to my mother, who hadn't moved during the entire ordeal. Her face was even more blank now, and her eyes were glassy.

"What should we do?" Ayla asked, her eyes wide.

It started again.

The earth shook harder and I could hear screams coming from the party.

"We need to get everyone out!" Ami said. "Come on!"

She grabbed my hand and pulled me toward the door, but I hesitated. "What about Mom?" I asked.

Aunt Gwennie looked up at me. "I'll take care of her, don't worry. You go with your sisters and make sure everyone gets out safely."

I hesitated for a moment longer before following Ami and Althea out into the hallway. The earthquake was getting stronger, and it was hard to keep my balance. People were running in all directions, screaming and bumping into each other in their panic. The ground shook, and I fell.

Ow!

I raised my head, but...I saw nothing threatening.

No monsters.

No ghosts.

No crazy magic energy.

Nothing.

I sprung to my knees and redoubled my efforts, clawing at the carpet as I tried to gain traction. Once back on my feet, I rushed back toward the alcove, then dove across the room and stretched my hand toward the pedestal that no longer held the toy soldier…

And then everything went black.

* * *

I've been on rides that performed simple illusions that could be mind-blowing.

You know the kind. You stand in a room and the lights go out. The room falls into pitch black darkness. Seconds later, light floods it once again and the re-illuminated space looks different from how it did a few moments before. It's as if you've been teleported or transported to a different location even though you never moved an inch.

When I opened my eyes, it seemed like that.

Only I was pretty sure we'd moved more than an inch.

"Where...are we?" Ayla whispered, in a hushed tone, as if something—or someone—was lurking around us. She twisted her body to look around, trying to get a good view of the place.

"Not in Kansas anymore," Althea said sardonically.

"I know this place," Archie mumbled.

"Where is it?" I asked him.

"I don't know, but I swear, I know this place somehow."

I stood guard over my three sisters. Archie crouched on my shoulder, monitoring them. I could feel his body heat emanating against my neck as his little heart pounded with anxiety. Four werewolves in wolf form stood behind, heads bowed, ears erect. They were clearly on alert, too.

Everyone else?

Everyone else was gone.

Our house was gone.

The party was gone.

Aunt Gwennie and Mom were gone.

Just...gone.

But where were they?

More important, where were we?

The ground was slightly transparent, as if it was water. Thousands of flickering lights illuminated the gloom, which made it feel like I was surrounded by fireflies. The fog was so thick, hugging the ground and mixing with the shadows almost seamlessly.

"I think we were brought here," Althea said slowly. "But I don't know why or by whom." She made a face. "Wherever we are, it's awfully humid. And keep in mind, I'm saying that as a lifelong resident of Central Florida."

I desperately tried to step forward, but it felt as if I were wading through water. Every movement was sluggish.

"Astra, don't," Ami said. My sister then reached into her pocket and grabbed her tarot deck. "I have my cards. We may as well use them to figure out what on earth is going on here." She shuffled the cards before placing them on the ground in front of her. As her fingers touched the deck, there was a brilliant flash of light and an image appeared in front of us.

"What does this mean?" Althea asked as she stared.

Four women stood in a semi-circle around an owl, four wolves at their sides. Nine faceless beings hovering over the Magician card at the base of the image. "The Magician," Ami said slowly. "We can shape our own destiny here. That's what it says to me. And...it seems like we've been brought here for a reason."

"Wow, sis, I could have told you that," Ayla said with an eye roll.

"I said that already, you know," Althea added.

Ami glared at Ayla and Althea. "You have anything to add that can help us, or did you just want to give me an attitude about who stated the obvious first?"

Ayla closed her mouth and held out her hand toward Ami.

"Thank you." She shuffled the deck once more, her eyes narrowing in concentration. Then she drew out three cards and placed them on the ground before us. "I will never be able to get this stuff off my cards."

The werewolf standing next to her huffed.

"The first," she intoned. "Is the Tower card. It means chaos, change and disruption—and it's also god-struck, so that tracks with what's going on. The second is the Star card—hope, renewal and light. Or you, Astra. And last...the Moon card." She shivered a little, a look of fear flashing across her face as she stared at it for a moment longer before continuing.

"That's good, isn't it?" Althea asked her.

"Not here, I don't think. I'm getting illusion, madness, fear, and confusion," Ami said quietly. "Who knows what any of these things mean here?" She gathered the cards up and placed them back in her pocket, standing up. "I think we need to be careful moving forward—wherever that may be. We don't know what awaits us in this strange new world we have found ourselves in."

CHAPTER FOUR

We walked, slowly, through the pearly haze that seemed to thicken with each shuffling step we took. Four werewolves and four witches were transported to wherever this was—but not all the werewolves, and not all the witches. My mother and Aunt Gwennie weren't with us. Eddie, too, apparently remained back at Arden House with Emma.

The haze cloaked over my senses like a fog.

In the blink of an eye, Lothian was right next to me. "You have to know where we are," he said as the other three werewolves with him—Wyatt, Norden, and Lawrence—also shifted back into their human forms. They flanked his tense stance with friendly looks on their faces.

"I don't have to, and I don't know," I told him.

"I wasn't talking to you." Lothian pointed to the right of my head. "I was talking to your bird there. We all came here when you touched the pedestal of that toy, and that toy was meant for the bird."

Butterflies flitted past me, their iridescent wings shimmering. I felt Archie tense to grab one as it flew by. "Don't," I cautioned him. "We don't know where we are, and we don't know what they are."

"Did you bring any of that jerky?" he asked.

"Archie, focus." Althea looked pointedly at him and then turned back to Lothian. "What's your point?" she asked.

"This has to do with that toy's threats against the bird," Lothian said, his tone a careful one, like he was trying to gauge Althea in some way. "We're just along for the ride, but it's clear to me that Bird here has to know where we are if this really is all about him."

"Would you stop calling me 'bird' like it's a proper name?" Archie shook his feathers and thrust his broad head toward Lothian. "If I called you werewolf, would that sound respectful? Or if I called them 'witch' or—"

"He has a name, you know," Ayla said with a

huff. "It's Archie. And he's right, it's not respectful to just call him 'bird.'"

The other werewolves looked at each other and then back at Lothian with bemused expressions.

Lothian sighed and rubbed his temples. "Look, we don't know what's going on here. But it's clear that the toy is after Archie for some reason, so it also stands to reason that he—Archie—might be our best bet for figuring out where we are and how to get back home."

"If that's the case," Ayla said, crossing her arms over her chest. "Stopping to school you on manners you should already know was a colossal waste of time. So how about you just act like a grown-a—"

"Ayla!" Ami said sharply.

"Look, I don't care what Fuzzball McMoody thinks. He's wrong. I do not know where we are, and I do not know what I'm supposed to do here. If anything." Archie's talons dug into my shoulder. "These divine tests don't come with a handbook, you know."

"No, I don't know," Lothian responded with a snide tone. "That's why I'm asking."

"You're not asking," I said. "You're demanding."

Lothian shrugged. "What's the difference?"

"The difference is that one asks a question and hopes for an answer. The other demands an answer and expects it to be given because of some misplaced sense of entitlement," I told the werewolf. Archie hopped up on top of my head and clicked his beak. "And to be honest, you didn't even demand. You pronounced a conclusion you'd come to. Based on what, though, I have no idea."

"You get used to the way he talks, eventually," Wyatt Marlow told me with a half-smile. "I don't think he means anything by it. He's just an abrasive—"

"He means everything by it, and you know it," Lawrence interjected.

"Lawrence," Lothian said in a warning tone.

"Oh, don't even start with us," Norden said to Lothian. Turning to Wyatt, he added, "Don't prop up the guy who's wrong, Marlow." Norden waved Wyatt quiet. "You're always defending him."

"I'm not wrong," Lothian deadpanned.

"I'm not propping him up," Wyatt countered. "I'm just saying that—"

"Guys," Ami said, trying to interrupt their argument, but failing. They bickered over her protestations. "Stop it. We need to—"

"Would you shut the hell up?" Althea shouted, her voice cutting across the foggy void. "We can't start fighting among ourselves."

"Start?" Archie whispered.

I shushed him.

"We need to stay positive and keep the peace in our own numbers." Althea looked around the group—stopping to glare at Lothian as she did so. "We have no idea where we are, why we're the ones here, and our 'travel benefactors' have left us alone with no instructions." She held up her phone. "We have no way of communicating with the outside world, and we don't know what we're going to face. I don't know about you guys, but I don't think the nine of us arguing helps anything."

"We should let the owl fly around," Wyatt changed the subject immediately. "Maybe he can sense some kind of—"

"No," Althea said before I could react.

"I mean, we should let him fly off—"

"No," Althea repeated, staring right at Wyatt. She held her ground, her eyes locked on him. I almost expected Wyatt to look away first, but he didn't; he stared right back at her, his arms crossed. "Archie's in danger. The star card said he was in danger." She glanced at Archie.

"Archie stays with us. You want to look around? You go."

The group fell silent, only to be broken by the sound of a chuckle from behind us.

I spun around to see a tall and slender cloaked man standing fifteen feet behind us, his features obscured by the hazy wisps of fog. A star-topped rod of smoky crystal was clutched loosely in his right hand. A deep hood obscured his features.

"Hello?" Ami called.

The figure continued standing there, calmly watching us.

"Who are you?" Ayla asked.

"Forgive my laughter. I did not intend to startle you," a man's voice said. It was full and warm, and it resonated with a friendliness that seemed familiar. "Your sister, Astra, is indeed a powerhouse. And at such a young age! Marvelous."

Huh.

"You know my name. Do I know yours?" I asked, walking toward the figure.

I know.

Approaching a hooded figure wielding a large magic stick in a smoky location where I'd been kidnapped isn't the most impressive move I've ever made. I have no idea why I did it. Maybe it was instinct. Something in my gut told me he was someone I should put my trust in. The voice reminded me of someone I couldn't quite place...

"I'm disappointed you don't remember me, Astra," the man said. "After all, we had a holiday together just recently." He drew his hood back.

No way.

He was aged slightly but still handsome, with a well-chiseled face, high cheekbones, an aquiline nose, and a rich voice. There was that same confident gleam in his eye.

And that smile.

I could not forget that smile.

"You're quite a ways away from Palm Beach," I told the god.

"Ah. Yes, good." He smiled, looking genuinely happy. "You remember."

"Palm Beach? Astra, who is this guy?" Ayla asked.

"Dr. Dell Loxias of Palm Beach. At least that's how humans know him," I replied, raising an eyebrow. "Who once told me he'd never kidnap anyone—but I'm starting to suspect wasn't telling me the whole truth last year."

"Astra." Dr. Loxias sounded disappointed.

"Last year?" Ayla asked slowly.

"Like a year ago when you went to Palm

Beach? That last year?" Ami asked, her eyes wide. "When we had the Orphic priest and…" Ami looked at Dell.

"Loxias," Althea said. Her finger tapped against her thigh in an odd pattern as she gazed at the strange man. "Loxias the obscure, I take it?"

Dell smiled and nodded.

"Also known as Lykaios?"

He nodded again, with a smile that grew all the wider, and exclaimed, "Yes! Yes!" His radiant expression reflected the pride he felt at Althea's recognition of him.

She turned toward Lothian. "You have no idea who he is, do you?"

"Should I?" Lothian asked.

"Well, he's the wolf god, so, yeah, maybe. Man, if you don't wind up in Tartarus instead of Archie, I'll be shocked." Althea held out her hand as if Dell Loxias was an old friend of hers. "Lothian Pennington, meet the god Apollo—master of wolves."

* * *

"THERE IS NO MASTER OF WOLVES." Lothian's eyes widened.

"Oh, I'm pretty sure there is," Althea replied, her tone serious. "I wouldn't joke about that. "

"She's right," I added. "Emma, Eddie and I spent last Christmas with him. Well," I said, tilting my head. "Sort of. It's kind of a long story."

"Apollo Lykaios is one of his full names, and he was worshipped as a wolf god at Mount Lykaion." Althea turned back around and held out her hand again. "Glad to meet you, Dell. I'm a big fan."

"I thought that was Zeus Lykaios," Ami said. "Assertions that Apollo had an archaic wolf form…are…um, speculative." Ami bowed her head sheepishly to Apollo. "No offense meant."

"None taken. But nope," Dell disagreed cheerfully. "Not speculative at all."

"There is no master of wolves," Lothian insisted again.

"That's not what Danaus said," Althea told him.

"Who the heck is Danaus?"

"Son of Belus, king of Egypt, and twin brother of Aegyptus. He became the king of Argos. Anyway!" Apollo clapped his hands together as if to shut the book on the debate. "I'm so happy to meet Astra's sisters—truly. Are you hungry?" Dell asked, turning his attention away from Lothian.

"My apologies; I meant to prepare you some snacks." He reached into an inside pocket of his cloak and held up what appeared to be a family-sized bag of popcorn. "Does this work?"

"Delicious," Ami said, grabbing a handful. "I love popcorn."

Lothian shot her a look I couldn't quite decipher, but she was already munching away.

"You brought us here to offer us snacks?" I asked, my brow furrowed in confusion.

"No, Astra." Apollo smiled. "I didn't bring you here at all. When I stopped in to your mother's party, though, I overheard everyone talking about what happened to all of you. I wanted to wish you a happy holiday, so I followed you here."

"Okay, hold up—where is here?" I asked Loxias.

Dell twirled on his heels and threw his arms out. The fog dissipated; the thick white mist rolled back against a previously unseen forest.

I gazed up in awe as a colossal temple came into view on the hilltop to the south of us. The structure was made of glistening white marble, which reflected a shimmering light off its polished columns and striking engravings into designs so intricate that I assumed it was arcane geometry. It was breathtakingly beautiful, its soaring columns and intricate carvings seeming almost otherworldly.

"Nice," my unimpressed sister replied politely. She gave Apollo a sidelong glance before raising an eyebrow. "That was cool and all, but it wasn't an answer," Althea stated.

"I'm glad you said it; If you hadn't, I was about to," Ayla grumbled.

"It must be a holy place," Norden said breathlessly. "I wonder who built it and why."

"Ask the self-proclaimed god if you're so keen to know. Obviously." Lothian said this with scorching condescension before turning accusingly toward Apollo. "Who's temple is that?" Lothian demanded.

If the nine of us died from this little adventure, I was sure it would be because of something Lothian Pennington said.

"My goodness, you're quite the puffed up pup, aren't you!" Apollo laughed cheerfully and ruffled Lothian's hair like the arrogant werewolf was a young boy. "I wondered how you werewolves would react to me without your alpha to give you cues, and yet you're as stout and sturdy as a castle wall, aren't you?" He glanced at the other three. "They follow your lead, do they? Goodness, what trouble you four must get into."

"You have no idea!" Archie muttered in a mocking tone.

Lothian visibly bristled with anger and frustration as he stared across the clearing at Apollo. The werewolf was clearly offended by the wolf god's friendly, but presumptuous, behavior. Suddenly, his demeanor changed, and Lothian seemed to decide he would not let the god get away with it.

"I asked you a question," Lothian said as he stepped forward. "I expect an answer. Is that your temple? Someone's temple?"

Lothian approached Dell fearlessly.

Yet with each step he took toward Apollo, the god seemed to gain another muscle, inch, or piece of strategic armor so large it might have been manifested just to intimidate. By the time Lothian was five feet away from him, Apollo appeared terrifyingly powerful.

The werewolf slowed.

He slowed again.

Finally realized he had severely underestimated Apollo's defensive ability, Lothian abruptly halted his advance. Apollo merely laughed kindly in response and returned to his original gentle appearance.

"You're lovely, fierce creatures, as you were

meant to be. I created you to be the perfect hunters, and you are. You are strong, fast, and agile. You have heightened senses and sharp claws and teeth. You are brave and fearless. You are exactly what I wanted when I created you."

"And yet we are not perfect," Wyatt said, his voice laced with sadness.

"Wyatt!" Lothian snapped.

"Sheesh, werewolves can be maudlin," Archie whispered.

Dell nodded in agreement and smiled fondly at Wyatt. "No, you are not perfect. You are flawed and imperfect, just like every other living creature. But that is what makes you so special. Your flaws make you unique and interesting. They are what make you who you are."

"Why did you create us?" Norden asked, his tone reverent.

Dell smiled proudly, as if the question had pleased him. "To protect the innocents of the world, of course. There are evil forces at work in this world, and I needed creatures that could stand up to them. That's where you come in. You are the protectors of the world, and I am so proud of you."

"Why would the god of the sun want to create

werewolves?" Lothian asked. "It makes little sense. We're nocturnal."

"You're crepuscular—typically more active at dawn and dusk. Anyway, it doesn't have to make sense," Dell said with a shrug. "I'm a god. I can do whatever I want."

Lothian continued to stare at Apollo, as if unsure of what to do. The other werewolves were also staring at the god, their expressions ranging from awe to fear. "So, what now?" Lothian asked.

Dell smiled and clapped his hands together. "Now, my dear boy, you need to protect this owl from whatever is coming to take its place."

* * *

"Take who's place?" I asked.

Archie looked confused. "My place? To take my place?"

"Of course. Hadn't you figured that out?" Apollo asked Archie.

"Not exactly, no," Archie replied. I watched as Archie seemed to shrink under Apollo's gaze. His mocking demeanor vanished, and he was filled with fear and apprehension. "I have no idea what you're talking about."

"As interesting as all this is, you still haven't

told us whose temple that is across the way, who brought the nine of us here, and why you really came here," I said, crossing my arms. "It's very good to see you, Dr. Loxias, but I have to tell you —I remember meeting you last year, and nothing about it was straightforward. I don't buy that you just 'swung by.'"

"Last year…oh, wait. The kidnapped panther?" Ayla asked.

I nodded. "And let's remember that 'kidnapped' should be used in the loosest of terms," I reminded Ayla and my other two sisters, who were listening closely and watching. "I don't want to say I don't trust you, sun god, but I find it hard to believe the four werewolves just happened to show up here with us, and then you —master of wolves—coincidentally showed up a few minutes later. So, come on, spill it."

"Spill what?" he asked, his eyes twinkling.

"Oh, man, I hate riddles," I muttered with annoyance.

"Boy, are you in the wrong mythology, star girl," Althea quipped.

I looked toward Ami, who'd been generally quiet and now seemed deep in thought. "You want to pull a card and see if you can get us any information about what's going on?"

"I already did, remember?" She shrugged. "We know we can figure this out, and we know some things presented to us won't be precisely the truth."

"And some things, like Dr. Dell here claiming someone wants Archie to be replaced, could be clues," I murmured. I turned to face him. "Come on, Apollo, get on with it," I said, my voice stern. "Just tell us what you meant."

"Astra, you are quick," he said, his eyes locking on mine. "Quicker than last year. I'm quite proud of you."

"I don't know if I should be offended or complimented by your assessment," I said dryly.

"Okay, let's take stock of what we know one more time." Ami shoved the bag of popcorn at Lothian and paced. "The toy soldier was enchanted by someone, and sent to us to issue an unspecific challenge to Archie. They claim its Athena, but Athena also sent me a star card, sparkled it, and stuck it on Archie—so she clearly wants us to keep him alive."

"Would he be dead if sent to Tartarus?" Norden asked.

"Souls are judged after death in Tartarus, so yes—Archie would have to be dead."

The owl swallowed loudly.

"I still say that Athena wanting him judged but not wanting him dead makes no sense, Lothian said. "It's two diametrically opposed outcomes."

"Unless she's willing to risk his life for all of us to work together," Ayla pointed out. "It's not the first time the gods set up a perilous lesson with the risk of damnation or death just to get a point across, right?"

"That's if Athena sent the soldier and sent the star card," Althea said. "We're assuming that the talking Chucky doll is from Athena—that's a heck of an assumption when we've never seen it before, we have no real proof she sent it, and we have proof that Athena wants Astra to protect Archie."

"It showed up the same way Archie did, though, and it made it through the wards." I turned on Apollo and pointed south. "Wait a minute. You still haven't answered the question. Who's castle/palace/whatever is that?"

"What, that?" Apollo asked innocently. "Can't you tell?"

I narrowed my eyes at him. "No, I can't."

"Look closely."

The image of the castle seemed to shimmer even closer to us on the horizon—or we all moved closer to it. I couldn't tell which.

It was even more obvious that it was not part of our world—the architecture was too Grecian, and aside from the geometric etchings, it was adorned with what looked like ocean creatures. Fish swam on the turrets, and coral and sea plants crawling up the walls and columns. The banners that flew from the towers were made to look like seaweed. Even the drawbridge had a giant octopus carved into it.

"Ocean themed…"

"Yes. That is the home of Poseidon," Apollo said solemnly. "And he will not be happy to see you, I fear."

CHAPTER FIVE

*A*lthough he was certain Poseidon would not be pleased to see us, Apollo sauntered the nine of us in without knocking.

The air inside the door tasted like salt and sand, seaweed and fish. The walls were lined with ancient seashells, sparkling gems and gleaming pearls, and every surface was charmingly decorated with artfully carved sculptures of sea creatures.

"Nice place," Lothian said. "What's Poseidon again?"

Ami looked surprised. "You don't know who Poseidon is? Really?"

"I know vaguely who he is." Lothian looked at the wall, squinting at a particularly large pearl.

"Something about oceans, right? He carries a big fork?"

"A trident. Poseidon is king of all the sea creatures," Althea said distractedly, her head swiveling on her neck to take in the place. "Ruler of seas, rivers, water, storms, tempests, winds, hurricanes, rain, floods, drought, earthquakes and horses."

"Horses?" I asked.

"Yeah, unexpected, right?" Archie said.

"Yes. Horses. And probably some other things I'm forgetting." Althea tapped her finger on her chin, making a pensive face. "But he's not the god or king of fog as far as I know, and this whole place seems to be made of fog. Well, outside this house. So where are we?"

Apollo smiled. "Of course he's the king of fog. What is mist but a cloud of tiny water droplets suspended in the atmosphere—"

"A ha!" Althea jumped on Apollo's statement and snatched the initiative. "What atmosphere? Earth's atmosphere? Are we still on earth?" A rustle of wind and waves, a ship's horn, a lightning strike and thunder sounded low in answer to her rapid questions, and she glanced around, confused. "Where is that coming from?"

Apollo pointed up.

We all looked up.

The painting on the dome ceiling depicted a stormy sea, and the intricate detail of the painting was incredible. I could see the texture of the ocean foam, the froth of the water, and the waves as they rolled toward the bumpy shore. Suddenly, a gigantic wave rolled across the room above our heads from one side of the light ring to the other as I stared.

"Well, that's different," Ayla murmured.

I lowered my gaze and turned to look at the draped windows. They were pulled closed as if to darken the room, but there was a mysterious light, just a sliver, between the fabric and the wall. As I approached the glass panels, the air grew cooler and the drapes parted at my touch.

I gasped.

We were—all of us, the castle or temple or whatever it was—beneath a vast ocean. The water was calm and clear, but it was teeming with life. Huge schools of fish darted through the water, colorful coral clung to the seafloor, and sleek sea creatures swam among them all. I watched in awe as a massive manta ray glided by.

"Astra, what do you see?" Ami asked me.

"What don't I see?" I muttered.

I could hear a chorus of whale songs echoing

through the thin, clear panes, and the salty tang of seawater in the air seemed to grow stronger the closer I got to the window.

"Oh, no. No way. No way," Archie said with a nervous glance. His talons gripped my arm as the owl's posture stiffened and his ear tufts stood straight up. "I hate water. I have no defense in the water. And once I'm wet—"

"I know, buddy. We're okay," I told him reassuringly, but my reassurance had exactly zero impact on the owl's anxiety.

"No!" he repeated in a high-pitched whine. The frightened owl's head swiveled toward my face. "Look, I'm fond of you and all, but if this stupid test involves that ocean out there? I'm dead. Drowned bird. Soggy fowl. Sodden winged thing. Whale food. Winged casualty—"

"Archie—"

"Squishy bird. All cawed out. I know that you're a little challenged on the mythology knowledge, but if Poseidon is involved in this?" Archie's little heart was beating so fast that I could practically feel it in my arm where his talons clung to me tightly. "You can just stuff me for Thanksgiving."

"Archie—"

"He hates Athena. Ever since that stupid

Athens thing." Archie puffed out his chest. "That means he hates me."

"Archie—"

"Astra," Ami whispered while tugging on my arm. "Look."

Now, to be honest, the presence of Poseidon was palpable as soon as I stepped into his domain. The salty, earthy scent of the ocean filled the air, and I could feel the power of the water god radiating from almost every corner of the room. And I'd been in the presence of gods before —I mean, I had a god power living in my gut.

Gods didn't intimidate me.

Heck, a year ago, I didn't even believe they existed.

The sight of King Poseidon himself, though, momentarily stunned me. Just for a moment.

"Uh... um..." I stumbled over my words.

Archie slapped his face with his wing. "You can't bumble like that during your first meeting with a Greek god," Archie scolded me. "You'll insult him."

I saw him standing against one of the walls, his arms folded, his expression indifferent. He wore a crown of seashells, and his long, sandy-blond hair was braided with seaweed. His eyes were a kaleidoscope of colors, shimmering mirrors reflecting the endless ocean itself, and his skin sparkled with the color of sea glass.

Apollo stepped forward and bowed low. "Lord Poseidon," he said in a voice so deep I could feel it rumble in my chest. "I bring you greetings from Palm Beach."

I blinked.

"The Lord of the Sea," Althea bowed as she dropped to her knees. "Thank you for welcoming us into you home."

Ami and I glanced at one another in surprise. Since when did Althea become some genuflecting god worshipper?

"Um. Yeah," Ayla offered with a curtsy. "The King of the Horses. Thanks. Cool place you got here."

Ami curtsied silently.

The wolves and Apollo stood tall and stared.

His face had the characteristic beauty of the gods—perfect, angular, with stunningly brilliant eyes and the tiniest, most imperceptible lines around his expressive mouth. His eyes glistened as he looked us over, lingering on me for a moment.

"Say something," Archie hissed.

I simply nodded. "Poseidon."

My owl gave a stuttering intake of breath. "My

fault. I said something," he whispered to himself. "I should have been more specific."

Poseidon's eyes flared with surprise, and his lips quirked in a half-smile. "Relax, Archimedes. I know who Astra is." He tilted his head as he met my eyes. "You are not afraid?" he asked, his voice low and rumbling.

"Nope." I shook my head. "You're just a guy."

Lothian peered at me with his sapphire blue eyes, his face locked in a look of immense shock. I sensed he was surprised—and impressed—by my casual response to the immensely powerful water god.

Archie, however, was not impressed.

In fact, the small owl shook with fear. "I'm gonna die," he whispered brokenly. "You're going to get me killed. Do you have any idea how hot Tartarus is? I don't even like the Florida heat."

"You're fine, Archie," I told him, and scratched his head.

"The owl truly is wiser than you, I think," Poseidon laughed. It was so deep and booming that it shocked me. "I am just 'a guy' to you?"

"Well, so, here's the thing," I said, shifting my weight from one foot to another. "Who's more powerful—a god, or the person who controls a god?" I patted my stomach. "My lightning power tells me I don't need to genuflect to too many people."

"She picks now to grow a spine about her powers?" Ayla asked with a concern.

Althea gave an uncomfortable chuckle.

Poseidon did not laugh.

The god's expression turned stony. "Is that so?" His deep voice carried an echo of the roar of distant waves against rocks.

The wind kicked up, gently blowing our hair and clothing. Just when I thought a confrontation would erupt between me and the king of all water, he turned abruptly toward Apollo.

"How is the oracle?" Poseidon asked Apollo politely. The god's face was relaxed and pleasant, but his eyes were cold.

I watched the two, not sure what to make of their interaction.

"Ah," Apollo said in a choose-your-words tone. "She, uh—she's doing well," Apollo answered with a friendly smile. "In fact, she was the one that mentioned I might want to join the little shindig you have going on."

That the water god had 'going on?'

So Poseidon had something to do with this.

"Did she?" Poseidon asked. "High priestesses are always getting in the middle of things they probably should stay out of." He glanced at me. "Wouldn't you agree?"

Before I could answer, Apollo responded.

"I'm sure they're all doing the best they can," Apollo said, also glancing at me. He was smiling, but I could see a flash of unease in his eyes.

The god tilted his head slightly toward Archie, and the look on his face made my stomach clench. "And now," Poseidon's voice echoed through the room, "we begin."

* * *

THE SEA-GREEN EYES of the god king glowed. The wind grew stronger within the castle/temple, whipping my hair around my face. Outside the window, the sea raged, and I was certain a storm was on its way.

Archie looked like he was about to faint.

"Wait!" Apollo shouted, jumping forward and holding up his hand. "Lord Poseidon, I request permission to speak!"

The wind slowed, then stopped.

The water calmed.

It became still for a moment, as if the world itself held its breath to hear the god's answer.

After what seemed like an eternity, Poseidon

turned his head toward the sun god. "I know your oracle prophesized you would be useful here, but…you're not. Return to Delphi."

"I live in Palm Beach now," Apollo told him.

"I don't care where you go."

Archie turned and stared at me, his feathers drooping. "He's going to kill me."

"No, he's not," I told my owl.

"He's going to kill me," Archie insisted, clutching my arm with his razor sharp talons.

"There is no way any of us are going to let that happen, Archie," I told the owl, who looked like he was about to have a nervous breakdown. "Athena never would have flashed that star card on you if she thought we couldn't defeat whatever was happening, right? So relax. We've got this."

My confidence wasn't as high as I led Archie to believe, but I would not let that pompous fork-waving overpowered merman overhear any of my nerves or concerns.

"Lord Poseidon?" Apollo prodded.

"Hmm?" the god asked distractedly as he stared at me.

"Can we talk?" Apollo glanced sideways at me. "Privately?"

"I will grant you that," Poseidon said with a nod.

A bubble of water descended from the ceiling and suddenly encased us in a silent, shimmering sphere. We were surrounded by the deep blue ocean, but it was clear as glass so we could see through to the other side as the two gods talked.

"Is this what your life is normally like?" Ayla asked. "And why do you have so many issues with water, Astra? First the fish hotel and now this."

"Hey, this isn't about me, remember?" I reminded her.

"Yeah, I wouldn't be so sure of that," Ami said. "They keep looking at you. So either it is about you, or they're super concerned about your ability to interrupt their plans."

"You think maybe this is about her?" Archie asked Ami. "Like Astra's the one at risk of going to Tartarus? Oh, what a relief." He tilted his head. "I could live with that."

I stared at the owl. "Gosh. Thanks."

"What?" Archie preened his feathers and let out a huff. "It's not like I want you to toddle off to the kingdom of Hades or anything. But, you know, if I had to make a list of people I'd like to see roasting over a spit and I had to put both of us on it? Well, I'd rather you be ahead of me." He shook his feathers. "No offense or anything."

"And you wonder why you keep getting effectively brought up on spiritual charges by the universe's empathy police," I told him.

"I'm immortal!" he squawked. "I've had eons to get comfortable with the idea that I'm never, ever, ever going to die. What do you expect me to do, just screw my head on differently? Embrace my sudden possible mortality?" Archie hissed. "Fat chance."

I kept one eye on the two gods outside the bubble. With frustration, Poseidon turned away, but Apollo grabbed his arm, talking all the while. No, not talking, I thought. Pleading. It looked like Apollo was pleading with the king of the sea.

"Astra, what do you think?" Althea asked.

"I think all nine of us got teleported to this seven seas fun house when only one of us was touching the pedestal base, so if I had to guess, I'd say this invite was for all of us and we're all at risk of something," I told her, and then jerked my chin toward the two gods. "Apollo knows something he's not telling us, and he's the master of wolves. Poseidon, as you know, has a history of having it out with Athena, and we belong to Athena."

"Okay, but what does that all mean?" asked Wyatt.

"I'd say just because the star card showed up for Archie doesn't mean this is only about him." I switched Archie from my right arm to my left. "It means that Archie's the only one Athena's concerned about dying."

Athena frowned. "You mean she'd be fine with the rest of us dying?"

"Oh, man, you know—she's right," Ayla said. "I never thought of it that way."

I shrugged. "I'm not saying that's what Athena would want, but it's not unrealistic to think she'd be willing to sacrifice a few of us to save the one. Archie being the one. Again, it's just a theory."

"Athena is that callous?" Lothian asked.

"Not callous. From everything I've tried to learn about her, she's not a villain," I told him. "She's a pragmatist. It wouldn't be a big deal to her if a few people died to save the one she really wants to save. There's a future purpose for everyone she picks for saving."

"What purpose?" Wyatt asked.

"I don't know. Maybe they're going to invent something important or save someone important or accomplish something history changing." I shrugged. "She doesn't send me a memo. Anyway, when trying to figure this out, it just helps to keep in mind these gods don't really care much about mortal death."

"Well, not yours," Archie pointed out.

Norden laughed, thinking Archie was making a joke.

He wasn't.

"From their perspective, death is just a change of form. They change form every Tuesday for tea on Mount Olympus. They don't see the big deal."

"Where does that leave the rest of us, then?" Lothian asked.

"In a water bubble," Archie told him helpfully.

As we stood there discussing the mystery of the teleporting toy and what the gods wanted from us, we were all acutely aware that we were facing real danger.

"Apollo clearly knows something," Lothian said.

"And Poseidon is clearly up to something," Ayla added.

Ami nodded her agreement. "As much as I know you have your issues with Athena, Astra, there is one thing I know for sure—Athena and Poseidon? They really don't like one another."

"How much don't they like one another?" Lawrence asked.

"Athena became the patron goddess of the city of Athens after a competition with Poseidon. He lost," Althea told Lawrence. " After the fight? Poseidon sent a flood to the Attic Plain, to punish the Athenians for not choosing him."

"Eventually though, he and Athena worked things out, and he helped Athena with the city of Athens," Ami reminded her. "But yes—they've had serious issues in the past, and there's no way to know what their relationship is like now. More often than not, they're at odds."

"And those two?" Lothian cut his eyes toward the two gods outside the water sphere, still deep in conversation.

"Well, Apollo helped him with the walls of Troy, but it's kind of complicated," Ayla said. "Apollo was on bad terms with Poseidon because of a dispute about payment for work. They had been sent by Zeus to work for the king of Troy for a year, but the dude refused to pay them at the end. They came to blows, but Apollo refused to fight. Poseidon thought Apollo was a coward for not fighting back and for assisting the Trojans."

Lothian looked impressed. "How do you know all this?"

"Our mother is the high priestess of Athena, remember?"

"Speaking of Mom," Ami said, her hand going to her hip and her finger tapping. "She looked really weird right before we left." She looked at me. "You were right across from her. Do you remember, Astra? I thought Athena had just bound her not to say something but what if that wasn't what was going on?"

"Poseidon, Zeus, and Hades are the three strongest gods," Ayla said with a look of growing concern. "Stronger than Athena. We've met Poseidon, we're being threatened with Hades' Tartarus...I wouldn't put it past them to mess with Mom if they're upset with Athena to keep Athena from warning us this is all a trick." She leaned forward and whispered. "And water dude holds grudges."

"Is this all a trick, though?" I wondered.

Lothian glared at me. "We were forcefully teleported, Astra."

"Yeah, okay. Good point."

* * *

FIVE MINUTES LATER, the water bubble surrounding us dissipated and we found ourselves in front of Poseidon again. "Greetings once more, mortals," Poseidon said in a booming voice. As he spoke, I got the sense he was sizing us up. As he did so, I felt a tingling awareness of unease as we stared back at him.

What did he want with us? And why had he brought us here, to this mysterious underwater realm?

Well.

If he had.

I didn't know if he had.

I knew little, if you want to know the truth.

And that bugged me.

I looked at Apollo, but he was expressionless and tight-lipped. His constant self satisfied little grin? Gone. Suddenly, the wordy therapist deity was silent.

What had the two talked about—and how did Apollo know to follow us here?

Did he follow us here?

Or was he part of whatever this was all along?

The doubts were climbing all over my brain now, and I wondered if Apollo had ever actually been helpful. Had he always been working against me? Was last year all a trick?

I didn't know.

And that was the worst part.

"Since the beginning of time, there have been two kingdoms," Poseidon said. "Mortals and immortals." He gestured to all of us standing in front of him. "I am an immortal. I am a god. You are mortal. You are not a god."

"Thanks, Captain Obvious," Archie whispered.

Poseidon looked at Archie. "But you are an immortal."

"If you can squash me like a bug, how immortal am I, really?" the owl asked him. "I thought I was, but it seems like every holiday, my gift is self-doubt and divine—"

"Archie!" Lothian hissed sharply.

"Sorry," the owl hooted.

"I am here to offer you a choice," Poseidon boomed. "A choice between two things."

What was this, now?

"Life and death," said Poseidon.

And that was when it all went to hell.

Literally.

CHAPTER SIX

"This is supposed to be Tartarus, right?" Ayla whispered as she turned around in what we all assumed was supposed to be hell— the opposite of Elysium, the deepest regions of the world, and the lower part of the two parts of the underworld. She surveyed our opulent surroundings. "I did not think hell would have a swimming pool."

"Yeah, I wouldn't jump in that if I were you," I told her.

"What is this, the friggin' DMV?" Althea complained as she leaned against the wall across from us. "We're just sitting here in a holding pattern, getting moved from waiting room to waiting room with no explanation and no idea where's next. Like I'm going in that swimming pool." She jumped as a wolf jostled into her. "Ugh, sorry."

"I'm with you," Ayla agreed. "I don't get this entire process."

"Hello there!" boomed a youthful male voice. It seemed to come from the very walls of the room.

Ayla let out a blood-curdling shriek as she stumbled backward and fell on the hard, cold, rocky ground. "Oh my gods, that scared me." Althea leaned forward, offering a hand. "Thanks."

"Rare a disembodied voice makes you jumpy," Ami said.

"Yeah, well, rare someone drops us into hell," Ayla countered. As she popped up, she looked over at the werewolves snarling and baring their teeth toward the pool. "What's up with them?"

"No idea," I said. "Maybe they sense something?"

The four wolves lined up as if on guard in front of us, their eyes glowing with an intense golden light. Their fur was thick and dark, with hints of gray streaked through it, and powerful muscles rippled beneath it.

I hadn't seen them as wolves often, and

despite my dislike of Lothian, even I had to admit they were striking creatures.

Well.

I didn't have to admit that out loud.

Suddenly, one wolf let out a fierce howl and charged toward the pool, his eyes blazing with intensity.

"Whoa, whoa, whoa," said the voice. "Boys, calm down. I will not cause you any harm."

Our mini-coven of witches, comprising Ami, Althea, Ayla, and myself, shifted nervously as we scanned the seemingly empty room.

"I'm not here to cause any trouble." A shadow shimmered at the water's edge, revealing that the voice belonged to a pasty-faced young man, possibly in his midtwenties, dressed in jeans and a white shirt. "I'm not sure what it is about this place and werewolves that makes them so touchy."

The four wolves prowled around us with a restless energy, their golden eyes glittering in the dim firelight of Tartarus.

"Who are you?" I asked as I looked around.

The valley we'd been dropped into was a deep, narrow canyon. It looked more like a crack in the earth than an actual valley—well, if this was earth, anyway. Outside the room and just above were various paths and bridges leading to other areas, and in the distance, I could see the tops of oddly designed buildings.

The large three-walled room we were in appeared to be cut out of the surrounding mountainous terrain on the canyon's right side. There was an opening to the canyon where the fourth wall should have been.

The room was…weirdly cozy.

A massive hearth burned a welcoming fire within the huge hearth in the corner of a room a few feet from a pristine pool that appeared to be chiseled from the rock floor itself.

The water sparkled and shimmered, reflecting the flames playing across the surface of the calm pool.

A large slab of white stone jutted out over it and provided comfortable seating, but white, red, and black lounge chairs were placed at various intervals around the pool if you wanted something cushier.

It was the type of place you'd expect to find on a cruise ship or tucked away on a wealthy billionaire's island.

Not Tartarus.

"I'm your tour guide of a sort," he answered, "and I'm here to answer any questions."

"Our tour guide?" I asked. "We get a tour guide?"

"Yes," he replied. "Who are you?"

I blinked.

Didn't he know?

"I'm…the leader of the group," I answered, not wanting to share my name with some random apparition in hell just yet.

Lothian barked in protest.

"Then shift back, dude," I told him. "You want to be in charge? You need to talk to people."

"How did you know what he said?" Ami asked.

"Because that's Lothian," I answered. "What else could he want?"

"Well, leader, let me bid you hello!" the apparition said as he waved at me. "Welcome to Hades. As I said, I'm here to help you."

"Okay," I responded. "Then help."

The place was a far cry from what I expected hell to look like. The walls were a lovely dark stone and had a pleasant glow—almost like sandstone, but not as light. Large tapestries hung from the walls in reds and whites and were the only other color in the place/ Well, besides the blue water in the pool. Everything was clean. No soot or black smoke as far as I could see.

"What do you mean, exactly?" he asked, smiling pleasantly.

Our tour guide was a ghostly figure, his pale yellow and white robes fluttering in a breeze I couldn't feel. The apparition was as tall as me, with a lean build, a long nose, and thin lips. Like a Grecian sculpture. His hair was dark and slicked back, his skin as white as paper.

"You were the one that said you're here to help. Help us with what?" I asked.

"Well, now, that's the question, isn't it?" He squinted at Archie. "Hello, Archimedes. How are you?"

"I'm in hell, you moron," my owl responded sharply. "How do you think I am?"

"Of course you are," the shade said with a friendly laugh. "Just remember, I'm here to help you." The young man tilted his head. "Are you sure you're the owl?"

"Are you kidnapping more than one today? If not, I'm sure," Archie said. "You're not much of a tour guide if you don't know who you're supposed to be helping."

"You're right, I should know who I'm helping. In any case, I'm glad to see you're in good spirits," the nameless young man replied as Archie muttered a few choice curses. The guide then turned to the werewolves. "And the rest of you, hello. I know you werewolves are touchy, but it's nice to see you, too."

"Why are you calling the wolves touchy?" Althea asked. "You've said that twice now, but only about the wolves. Not about us." She stepped forward, leaving a comfortable distance between herself and the young man. "Is there some reason that the wolves should be touchy?"

"The shifters don't like it when they get stuck in their animal forms," the young man explained.

"What?" she asked. "What do you mean?"

My eyes shot toward Lothian, who (now that I really looked at him) had an expression of pure misery on his face.

"It doesn't happen often, but when it does, it can be painful. I mean, it's not a big deal, especially not in the afterlife, but when someone is trapped in one form and they're not used to it, they get a little crabby."

Lothian's yellow eyes narrowed, and a low growl rose from deep within his chest. The wolf stared threateningly at the young man like a furry sword of Damocles while the young man simply smiled back at him in response.

"Trapped?" Ayla asked. "They're trapped?"

"What do you mean, 'blocked from shifting?'" I asked.

The tour guide turned. "It's not much more complicated than that. It means that they can't shift. They're stuck in their wolf form while they're here. If they were to shift, they would be much more dangerous. We don't want anyone getting hurt, so we…disallow certain things once mortals have crossed over here."

Right.

Hell management doesn't want anyone "getting hurt."

Like them?

I twisted my hand behind my back and made a fist. Focusing my attention on the gleaming white electric thread of mystical powers flowing inside me like a river, I tested whether my powers were still there. In response, a burst of energy erupted from my clenched hand, briefly lighting up the area behind me with an audible sizzling buzz.

Oops.

Althea jumped next to me. "Oh, goodness! Excuse me," she said, patting her hand delicately over a grimacing mouth. "I gorged on shrimp at the party. It always makes me gassy."

Ami stared at us wide-eyed.

"Of course. Noxious gas is nothing new down here, I assure you." The young man moved to the side of the pool and gestured toward the stone seats lining one wall. "Please, have a seat. You all seem to be holding up well, considering the circumstances, but I imagine it won't be long before the effects of being in Tartarus take their toll."

My sisters and I glanced at one another and then sat quickly.

The werewolves exchanged concerned glances, then reluctantly moved to sit down at the foot of our stone seats. To my surprise, Lothian sat down next to me. I could feel the tension radiating off him.

"What effects?" Althea asked him.

The young man smiled. "Tartarus has a way of wearing down mortals. It's hard to explain, but you'll feel it soon enough. You might feel tired, or hungry, even though you just ate. You might see things that aren't really there."

"Is there anything we can do to prevent these effects?" I asked him.

The young man shook his head. "I'm afraid not. Tartarus is a powerful place, and it takes a toll on everyone who comes here. Just try to remember that I'm here to help you, and that eventually you'll be able to leave." He looked at Archie. "Well. Most of you."

The owl looked stricken.

* * *

"You want us to watch a movie?" Althea asked in disbelief.

The screen, a great rectangle that filled the far wall of the pool room, burst to life with a crackling blue light. "Welcome to Tartarus!" the film began in the darkened pool room. "We're very glad you're here! Probably much happier than you are to be here!"

It reminded me of high school, sitting in the gymnasium and watching a health education film. Only this time, instead of learning about the birds and the bees, we were apparently going to learn about the monsters and the demons.

"Tartarus is a place for lost souls," the film continued, "and we have a lot of them!"

The image on the screen changed to that of a large cavernous room filled with thousands upon thousands of people. They were all shapes and sizes, and they all looked miserable.

"These are the lost souls," the voice informed us (in case thousands of miserable faces weren't obvious.) "They come here when they die, and they stay here until they've learned their lesson."

The image on the screen changed to that of a large gray wolf with yellow eyes. The wolf was pacing back and forth in a small enclosure, its head low and its teeth bared. It was clearly agitated.

Lothian whined quietly and pressed against my leg.

"Souls are not just human," the voice said as the camera zoomed in on the wolf. "Many creatures can make terrible decisions and wind up here! Paranormal creatures, animals, even plants!" The image changed to a large venus flytrap with its mouth open and saliva dripping. "So beware, all you creatures of the world! You never know when you might make a mistake and end up here in Tartarus!"

"Okay, this is horrifying," Althea murmured.

"But don't worry," the voice said cheerfully. "Tartarus is not a place of punishment. It's a place of rehabilitation. Eventually, all lost souls will find their way back to the world of the living."

The image on the screen changed to that of a beautiful woman with long blond hair and blue eyes. She was wearing a white dress, and she was surrounded by a group of merry, giggling children. With a wave, she turned and walked toward the sun, the children following behind her. "This is Persephone," the voice said. "Once a year, if you've learned your lessons well, you, too, can return to the mortal world and give it another go!"

"Who's that?" Althea whispered.

"Be quiet, I'm listening," Ayla told her.

The sunlight faded and the happy image changed.

The camera focused on a small girl with dark hair and green eyes. She was sitting in a large empty field, and she looked incredibly sad. "This is Lily, and Lily is a witch," the narrator said. "She made a wish that her family would disappear..."

The camera panned out to show that the girl was sitting in a large circle of ashes.

"And, as you can see, they did. Her story is not at an end, however! In Tartarus, Lily has a chance to understand herself," the movie continued as Lilly stood up with a determined look on her face. "We learn! We grow! We change! And eventually, we may leave."

"Yes, but how?" Archie snapped.

"Be careful what you wish for," the voice said as Lily faded to black. "You might just get it."

* * *

THE MOVIE CONCLUDED, and silence filled the theater for several seconds. Ayla muttered in shocked confusion as she tried to comprehend why we were shown the film. "I just...I mean..." Ayla looked at Ami.

"No idea. I'm speechless," Ami told our youngest sister..

"I know!" the young man exclaimed, clapping his hands together. "What an incredibly inspiring film!"

"Um...sure." Althea told the pallid young man, and then she leaned toward us. "I have to say, this is nothing like we were taught in home school. It seems Mom and Aunt Gwennie may have left a few things out."

I mulled over everything in my head, trying to come up with a zinger of a question for the anemic-looking guy that would illuminate everything. I reached out absentmindedly and scratched Lothian's head as if he were an actual wolf and not, you know, a completely annoying, arrogant werewolf with a superiority complex.

Unexpectedly, his enraged voice screeched through my mind as soon as my fingertips touched his fur.

"—and use your stupid magic to turn us back! HOW CAN YOU BE SO CALM! We're stuck! You—"

I pulled my hand away as if he burned me. "Oh, boy."

"Oh, boy?" Althea asked, her eyebrow raised.

Looking around at the other werewolves, I could see that they, too, were on edge. They shifted anxiously next to my sisters, glancing nervously at each other and at the young man leading us through the most uninformative information presentation I'd ever gotten.

And I was in the military.

I'd seen a lot of those.

"Look, I get it," I said, trying to calm the wolves down. "Honestly, I do—no one likes to have part of their identity just stripped away. I'm sure hell management has their reasons for blocking your shifting power, but even if they don't?" I held up my hands. "We just have to deal with it for now."

Lothian huffed at me and pawed the ground menacingly.

"Don't get sassy with me." I squinted at him. "Is that really helping?"

Lothian huffed at me once more and bared his long, sharp teeth.

My 'deal with it' message agitated the other werewolves, too, and I could feel impatience and anxiety radiating off them. They clearly wanted to do something other than sit back and accept the situation, but they didn't know what they could do.

I didn't, either.

I placed my hand on Lothian's neck once more, and once again his voice flooded my mind. "I am not some mindless animal to be caged and controlled! I will not be treated like—"

"Dude." I pulled my hand away.

He barked.

"Well, if you want me to listen, don't scream at me. I didn't do this to you." He bared his teeth at me. "No, you chill." I glared back at him (so long and so hard it felt like a millennium had passed) until he finally looked away.

Satisfied that I had—at least temporarily—quelled the canine mutiny, I turned my attention back to the young man claiming to be helpful. "So, what now?"

"Please let the wolves know that we're terribly sorry for their inconvenience," he said. "I'm sure none of you meant for this to happen, but it happens from time to time."

Hold up.

None of us meant for this to happen?

We all meant to be drinking Krasomelo (a Greek mulled wine popular around the holidays) and chomping down on those sweetened pitas my aunt always made this time of year. None of us planned to drop through some wormhole into Poseidon's living room, and then once more straight through to the bottom floor of hell.

"Excuse me," Ami said, holding her hand out toward me. "Is it permitted for you to let us know your name?"

"Of course!" He bowed. "I am Aeacus. You can call me Ace."

Wyatt stood up on four paws and barked twice.

"He's friends with Prometheus and Apollo, Astra," Althea whispered as she casually strolled by me. "He assisted them in building the walls of Troy." She turned on her heel and walked back by. "And after his death, he became one of the three judges here. He's the judge of Europeans."

I frowned. "What does he judge?"

"The deeds of the deceased."

Ace, obviously overhearing every whispered word, nodded. "That is correct. I also helped create the laws that govern the underworld," he told us proudly.

"And you're sure there's nothing we can do about the whole..." I gestured to the werewolves. "Shifting thing?"

"Unfortunately, no," Ace said. "It is beyond my power to change. I'd have to talk to my fellow judges and it's very difficult to get us together for a meeting. Zoom doesn't work down here." He brightened. "If you have a dead guy with European roots you need judged, though, I'm your guy."

Ayla snorted. "You must be busy."

I sighed. "I figured as much."

Lothian was especially vocal, pacing back and forth and growling under his breath at Ace's response. Finally, he turned to me, his yellow eyes boring into mine.

"Don't worry," I said to Lothian. "We're going to get through this—together." I nodded in sympathy, my eyes still fixed on the sleek werewolf.

He huffed.

"What about Hades?" Althea piped up suddenly. "Can't we go talk to him? Maybe he'll be able to help us. He is Athena's uncle, after all. The relationship between Athena and Hades is barely mentioned in mythology. Maybe they like each other."

All the werewolves turned to look at her, and even Ace looked surprised by the suggestion. "Hades?" he repeated slowly. "You want to go talk to…Hades?" She nodded. "Like, now?"

"Why not?" Althea asked with a shrug. "It's worth a shot, right? Besides, what have we got to lose?"

Suddenly, I was aware of just how young and idealistic my sisters could be, how deep we were underground, how far away from the surface we were—and the long list of things we had to lose.

CHAPTER SEVEN

*A*ce led the way down a mossy stairway, the soles of his boots slapping against the wet stone. The sound was like an off-key dirge, and it made me nervous about descending even further into this unknown space. I could feel the eyes of the werewolves as we walked—their expressions ranging from protective to accusatory—and I wondered what they were thinking.

I did not touch any of them, though.

I had no aspirin on me.

Anyway, I understood their unhappiness. A stranger—even one who looked to be on their side—wasn't someone they could trust by nature, and this was a hard thing for them.

Heck, it didn't come naturally to me.

But Ace seemed like our best bet at finding Hades, and Hades might be the only one with answers—so we had no choice but to follow his lead for now.

I mean, what was the alternative?

Wander around hell and look for a door?

I knew we'd find dozens of doors. Maybe hundreds of doors. I didn't want to open any of them just to see what was on the other side. Not in this place.

"Hades is…a bit of a recluse," Ace warned us as we walked. "He doesn't much like company. But if you can get him to listen to you, he might help." Ace didn't explain what he thought we needed help with. "Just be careful."

The path Ace lead us through was winding and treacherous, and more than once, I had to grab one of my sisters before she fell into one of the deep crevices that dotted the walls on either side of us. We walked for what felt like hours, our footsteps echoing in the vast cavernous divide.

"What was that?" Ayla whispered.

"Just keep your eyes forward and follow me," Ace responded without answering her question.

The long, dark ravine lined with torches

seemed to go on forever. I could hear water dripping and the occasional scuffle of rats or other small creatures as the flames flickered and danced ominously, casting eerie shadows on the walls.

"I can't believe I wore heels to that stupid party," Althea muttered, glaring down at her black wedge sandals. She glared at me. "And of course you're in combat boots."

"They're duty boots," I said with a shrug.

"Be careful climbing up, please," Ace said as he confidently ascended steps out of the narrow gorge.

I climbed up and out of the rocky crevasse behind Ami to find a stone archway, only visible because of the glow of the torches that lined it. The light was just enough to illuminate the outline of an iron door in front of me, framed and supported by wooden braces and marked by shining rivets that ran along its edges like teeth.

"That's quite a door," Ayla observed.

Ace produced a large key from his pocket and inserted it into the lock. There was a loud click, and then the door swung open with a creak. "I know he looks fierce, but he's really quite harmless to you. Just hold still and let him smell you."

"Hold up. Let who smell me?" Althea asked him, alarmed.

As we stepped through the door, a sudden and terrifying growl echoed across the cave. The members of my hellscape adventuring party and I froze in fear, and I could feel my heart pounding in my chest.

"What the hell was that?" Ayla asked.

Althea pointed.

A massive creature stood twenty feet in front of us—a three-headed hell hound with glowing red eyes and razor sharp, fang-filled jaws. The beast's teeth snapped and gnashed threateningly in our direction, and its breath wafted toward us like a hot wind.

"You've got to be kidding," Ami murmured, then cast an accusatory stare at Althea, which was unusual for her. "This was your idea, Althea. I'm totally blaming you for this."

"Don't look at me. I'm just trying to handle what the bird got us into."

"It was Astra that touched that pedestal," Ayla pointed out.

"Ladies, please! Just stay still and whatever you do," Ace warned, "don't run from him. If you don't run from him, Cerberus won't see you as a threat."

That three-headed dog was as big as a bus.

I wasn't worried about *his* fear factor.

The gigantic animal eyed us hungrily, its long tongue licking its sharp teeth as it watched our every move. Suddenly, Cerberus lunged forward and bared all three faces full of fangs at Ace, who stood firm before him without flinching.

"Easy now, boy," he soothed, holding out his hand to calm Cerberus' rage. "These are friends."

The hell hound sniffed in our direction warily, probing us for danger even as he seemed to recognize Ace's scent and grow calmer with each passing moment. Slowly but surely, Cerberus relaxed and the tension in the air slowly eased.

Well, in those on two legs.

The wolves continued to stare at Cerberus warily.

Two of his three heads stared back at the wolves curiously.

The wolves weren't sure what to make of this strange creature, with its fiery red eyes and razor sharp claws. They let out low growls as they circled the enormous dog, their hackles raised and their teeth bared in warning while cautiously creeping forward, their bodies low to the ground.

In response, Cerberus bounded toward them

playfully, a delighted grin spreading across his gleaming fangs on all three of his faces.

"Wait. What?" Ayla said in disbelief.

The wolves' paws skidded across the rocky ground as they wrestled with the enormous beast, their tails wagging and tongues lolling. The three-headed hell hound appeared to have a good time, rolling around on his back and barking at his new friends.

"Well, that went better than I'd hoped," Ace said with a relieved chuckle.

"I never would have guessed that Cerberus could be so...friendly," I drawled.

"Yeah, he's usually a bit of a grump, but he seems to have taken a liking to you guys," Ace replied. "Just be careful not to get on his bad side —those razor sharp claws can do some serious damage."

The wolves leaped at him, nipping at his belly and tugging on his thick fur. He barked and snapped in response, clearly enjoying their company as they wrestled and tumbled in the dirt.

* * *

WE CONTINUED on with one more (or three more, depending on how you looked at it) added to our party.

I marveled at the cave's surreal beauty as we passed through it. In the light of the torches, huge crystal formations glittered like stars against the black expanse of stone. The walls glistened with rushing waterfalls, and massive stalactites hung like frozen behemoths from the vaulted ceiling.

There was a strange energy in the air, an almost palpable sense of magic.

"It looks like space, kind of," Althea observed.

"You've been awfully quiet," I said to Archie.

He looked around nervously, his feathers fluttering as he scanned the cavernous expanse. "Something is going on here...something dark. It's lurking in the shadows. I can feel it. I don't think I've ever been so absolutely petrified in my life— yet I almost feel like this place is calling to me, imploring me to stay." Archie shuddered, his feathers vibrating. "Weird."

"Ace said we'd imagine things," Ayla pointed out.

"No, I said you'd see things," he disagreed. "I didn't say you'd feel things."

Ayla stopped walking. "Yes, you did. You said

we might be hungry even though we already ate. That's a feeling."

Cerberus barked happily three times in succession and sat back to extend his razor sharp front paws toward Ace. Then he whined loudly in triplicate.

Ace looked at the dog and then back at Ayla. "You're right, I said that. Of course, there are dark things here. This is the underworld." Ace fished a large juicy steak out of his coat pocket and presented it to Cerberus. The dog's eyes sparkled with glee as he snatched it from Ace and devoured it in two bites. "I'm glad I thought to bring an extra," he said with a chuckle, ruffling the dog's fur affectionately.

Cerberus whined again and scratched vigorously at the ground. The wolves, salivating, joined in with plaintive whines. Then he looked back up at Ace with an expression that said, "I want another treat!"

Ace laughed and ruffled the dog's head affectionately. "I have no more treats on me, buddy. Sorry."

Cerberus cocked his head to the side, considering this for a moment. Then he bounded off into the darkness, disappearing around a corner.

We all looked at each other, wondering what to do.

"Do we follow him?" Ayla said hesitantly.

"I don't know—" Althea began.

But before she could finish her sentence, a wolf-like howl pierced my ears and thudded against my chest like a pile-driver. I felt the rumble of its force to my bones.

"What was that?!" Ayla yelped, clinging to my arm.

Cerberus came bounding back around the corner then, looking slightly sheepish. A towering woman with angular features stormed around the corner behind him, her dress covered in a material that mimicked twinkling stars.

"Who is that?" I asked Archie.

He shook his head.

The woman held a knife of black steel in her hand, and her eyes burned red as she glanced at each of us. Her hair was black as night and braided intricately with silver pulled back from a face with skin like fresh alabaster polished to the most lustrous sheen.

"No idea who she is, but I want her skin care regimen," Ayla said under her breath. She sniffed. "Do I smell apples?"

The woman held up a box of apple-scented

candles with an aroma so strong I craved pie. A keyring in the shape of a trident dangled from her finger.

Ace bowed his head slightly. "Goddess, I—"

"Were you planning on bypassing my wing?" the woman asked Ace. The knife—brandished toward our tour guide—had an ivory handle with a blood red jewel embedded in the hilt. As menacing as she looked, the goddess spoke with a sweet, sultry voice.

I sensed being at ease around this woman was a mistake.

Althea's voice floated into Ace's frightened silence. "Wait a minute. I know you. I know her. That's Hecate," Althea whispered, the words sounding choked in her throat. "Guys, this is Hecate."

"Well, at least one of you recognized me," she said with a satisfied smile, tossing her sleek braid over her shoulder. "What Athena wants with a family of witches that should, by right, fall directly under my purview? I have no idea. Not that I ever bothered to ask her." She put her hand on her hip and the folds of her dress became like the stars in the sky, swirling and swirling. "Clearly, since you're here, she can't very well isolate you."

"Now, look here—" Archie started.

"Don't you dare defend your mistress to me, Archimedes," Hecate told him, her eyes flaring brightly. "I am Hecate, queen of the witches," she told him with a coy smile, batting her eyelashes. I felt a chill run down my spine. "You know very well what my domain is. She and I had an agreement regarding this family, their oaths, and your guidance—such as its been. It did not include dragging the four girls down here to Hades. Did it?"

"That's a nice knife," Althea said suddenly.

Hecate turned to face her. "This?" she said, holding the knife to showcase the jewel.

"Yeah, that's a cool knife," Althea said with a dreamy sigh.

Hecate laughed then, a low and husky chuckle that sent another shiver down my spine. She looked at Althea with an intrigued glint in her eye. "Do you want it, child?"

Althea gave her a wide smile and nodded eagerly.

"Althea," I warned, but my sister ignored me.

Hecate smiled at us all, a benevolent glint in her eye.

"Althea!" I warned her again, but she

continued to ignore me. "Don't accept a gift from a god without asking what it means!"

"Why not?" Althea asked. "You did."

So.

Okay, she got me there.

Hecate tossed her dark hair and smiled sweetly. "I am queen of the witches. I mean no witch any harm, Astra," she said in a honey smooth voice. Hecate chuckled once again, tossing the knife expertly to Althea.

My sister caught the dagger in mid-air, her eyes lighting up as she held it up to the light and admired its sharp blade and gleaming hilt. "Wow," Althea breathed. "This is a beautiful dagger. It's seriously amazing, Hecate. Thank you so much!"

Althea looked up to see Hecate smiling down at her.

"What's the price?" I asked coldly.

Hecate smiled in satisfaction and nodded. "Always so suspicious, Astra," she said proudly. "But Althea, your sister is right. Now that I have given my gift to you, young witch, I ask only one thing in return."

"What's that?"

Here it comes.

"An oath to honor me above all goddesses, and

to accept my guidance," Hecate said, her eyes gleaming wickedly. "Will you take my oath?"

Althea looked at me uncertainly, and I shrugged.

I couldn't decide for her.

"Um, wait a minute," Archie said slowly. He squinted and rubbed his feathered chin with his wing. "What form is your guidance taking?" Hecate ignored him. "Witch queen? I have a question."

But the witch queen had eyes only for Althea.

Finally, my sister nodded eagerly, her eyes full of excitement and reverence as she gazed upon the goddess. Before anyone could say anything else, she sank to her knees before Hecate and swore an oath of loyalty.

"Oh, boy," Ayla said, her expression troubled.

"Yes!" Althea repeated, looking up at Hecate with admiration and awe. "I will accept your guidance and honor you for all eternity. Thank you!"

I sighed.

Hecate smiled, her eyes crinkling in pleasure. She stepped back then, letting her hands slide from Althea's face to settle on her shoulders. "You are truly a worthy witch, my dear," she murmured in a low voice. "I will guide you on your path to greatness."

With that, the goddess disappeared in a puff of smoke, leaving Althea clutching the blood red jeweled knife tightly in her hand.

"Well, I didn't expect that," Ayla said.

"Or that," Ami exclaimed, pointing. "Look!"

The spot where Hecate stood was not empty when the smoke cleared.

"I knew it," Archie grumbled.

We were taken aback by a beautiful owl perched on the floor staring up at Althea. It was a lovely creature, with stunningly bright white feathers and golden eyes as bright as the sun.

"I don't understand," Althea whispered breathlessly, entranced by its beauty. The owl gazed upon her with wise eyes and ruffled its feathers slightly as she approached. It seemed to smile at her. "Is this Hecate?"

"No, it's not Hecate, you nitwit," Archie squawked, clearly annoyed that he wasn't the only owl available to assist the Arden sisters. Althea gently stroked the owl's feathers and whispered softly to it, and he seemed to become even more agitated. "The stupid bird doesn't even talk!"

A female voice cracked a response like a whip. "Of course I can talk, you arrogant barn owl—"

"I'm a great horned owl, you stupid—"

"From what I've heard, you're only a glorified owl decoy on your best day," the snowy owl hooted derisively. "I also understand that you don't have a lot of those and could probably use a superior divine animal to learn from. You know, so you don't make as many messes."

"Fine, we've gotten your message about not polluting, Albino Woodsy," Archie said in a surly voice. "You can go back to the Arctic now and save a polar bear or something."

The snowy owl merely chuckled and ignored my owl with a haughty toss of her head. "Ah, don't mind him," she said to Althea in a soft, musical voice. "He's just jealous because I'm so much prettier than he is. And smarter than he is. And more mature than—"

"You know, some owls eat other owls!" Archie shouted.

I looked at the two animals in wonder, my mind racing with questions I couldn't articulate in my surprise.

"Would you two please stop fighting?" Althea said, her brow furrowed in annoyance. "You're giving me a headache."

"Sorry, Althea," the two owls said in unison, looking contrite.

The snowy owl preened slightly and then fixed Althea with a piercing gaze. "Hecate has charged me with guiding you on your journey, young witch," she said solemnly. "And I will now that you are a priestess to the goddess you should have been priestessed to all along."

Archie squawked in offense.

"What's your name?" Althea asked the owl, ignoring Archie's indignant disapproval.

"My name is Lily," the owl said in a soft, musical voice. "I am Hecate's chosen animal, and I will be your guide from now on."

"Thank you, Lily," she said breathlessly. "I won't let you down."

"I know you won't, my dear," Lily said with a knowing smile. "Hecate has faith in you, and so do I."

A heaviness filled me. It was as if my mother were watching, scowling in disapproval already. I swallowed hard. I could feel her objection pressing down on me from the future like a heavy black fog.

Althea turned toward me. "So, wait, am I not a member of the coven anymore?" she asked, her voice concerned.

"I don't really know what this means, sis—but we'll figure it out."

Ayla and Ami agreed.

The snowy owl gazed at her with wise eyes filled with warmth and understanding, seeming to know exactly what was going through Althea's mind.

"Do not be afraid," Lily said gently, ruffling her feathers once more. "With me by your side, you will find your true path and fulfill your destiny as a powerful witch guided by Hecate." The owl gently cooed to her and nuzzled her cheek with its soft feathers. "You will be who you are meant to be."

"I see Lily already does not know what she's talking about, and she certainly has no clue about Minerva Arden," Archie muttered. He perched on my shoulder but was giving the snowy owl the most vicious side-eye. "I can't believe Althea rejected her family for a knife—"

"Stop," I told him, reaching back to transfer him from my shoulder to my wrist. He flapped in protest, but finally allowed me to move him so we could look at each other face to face. "You don't get to do that."

"What?"

"Say things like that about Althea's choices. At

least she had a choice. You and Athena manipulated me into becoming whatever it is I've become with this star stuff. Althea had a choice. And she made it."

"It's just hard to see her rejecting her family like that," he said immediately, looking contrite.

"She didn't reject her family. She made a choice for herself," I said, reaching up to stroke his head with my free hand. "Trust that she knows what she's doing. And maybe, just maybe, this is exactly what she needs to find her true path."

"Yeah. Okay. Sure. Hey," Archie asked, looking up at me. "You think that little speech is going to work on your mother, too?"

I looked over at Lily, who fluttered her brilliant white feathers while staring intently at Althea with her shining yellow eyes.

Nope.

That speech would not work on my mother.

CHAPTER EIGHT

"*J*ason must be worried sick," Ami said as we continued to walk deeper into the cave. "He's probably calling you every ten minutes, trying to figure out where you are."

Ayla nodded grimly and glanced about her, never meeting my eyes.

The strange and dreary cavern was lit only by fire pits set into the walls or along the corridor floor. The light smoke from the burning timber and coal swirled here and there, but never dispersed into the glum, wet atmosphere of the cave.

I pulled out my phone and confirmed once again there were no bars (well, mobile phone bars) in hell. "I'm sure he'll be fine. Mom and Aunt Gwennie can explain what's going on." With each step we took, my senses seemed sharper and more attuned; I could hear every tiny movement in the dark corners of the surrounding cavern.

"They may not have a clue where we are, either." Althea looked sideways at me. "You know, if your relationship is the ideal I have to aspire to, I'm not sure I want a boyfriend."

"We're going to talk about my boyfriend instead of the life-changing thing that just happened to you?" I pointed at the white owl. "Or what's happening to us? Yeah, sure. Let's do that." I rolled my eyes and sighed heavily. "Have at it."

"Well, it seems like you're always worried about what he's thinking or feeling, and whether he's happy. Honestly, Astra, it just sounds like a lot of work. And Jason is always worried about you, trying to control where you are and what you're doing. If I didn't know better, I'd say he doesn't trust you very much."

I frowned.

Sure, Jason had been more possessive than usual since we'd come back from the island, but I had assumed it was because our relationship was so rocky during that weird adventure. "I guess you could see it that way from outside," I intoned.

"But he trusts me, Althea. He just wants to keep me safe."

"Really?" Althea snorted. "If he trusted you, he wouldn't be so worried all the time. And he definitely wouldn't try to control where you go and what you do. That's not love; that's possessiveness."

"Knock it off," Ayla snapped. "I like Jason. He's a good guy."

"Then why don't you date him? You're more into him than Astra is," Ami quipped with a smirk.

"Because I'm sixteen, he's an adult, and he's dating my sister!" Ayla responded, struggling to keep her anger in check. "You know, just because you're eighteen now doesn't mean you get to be gross."

She stopped walking and looked at Ayla, then glanced at me, adding quickly, "I'm sorry. That was out of line."

Frustrated, I turned away and continued walking through the dark cave, my mind focusing more on getting us out of there rather than on my frustrating sister's observations about my romantic life. "Yeah, it's fine," I said without turning around. "Don't worry about it."

"See what I mean?" Althea spat out with

annoyance. "Astra just has no reaction where Jason is concerned. I mean, come on. That's not normal."

I glanced behind me to find Lily bobbing her head up and down to agree with her new mistress. "I'm sure you're right," she chimed in musically.

"Oh, yeah? I'm sure you couldn't even pick Astra out of a crowd. So maybe you should keep your uninformed opinions to yourself," Archie snapped back.

"It must be so hard serving a goddess that has no magic," Lily responded, her voice dripping with obviously false compassion. "I totally understand why you might be a bit intimidated by—"

"You're such a duck brain!" screeched Archie with rage.

The white owl opened her beak to say something, but Althea whispered just as she flapped her wings to launch across the bleak rock hallway at Archie.

Lily settled down and kept her beak closed.

"Althea, is this really the time and the place for this discussion?" Ayla hurried to catch up with Ace, who was leading us.

"Why not? All we're doing is wandering

around. Speaking of—hey, dude, are you sure this is the right way?" Althea asked skeptically, looking around at the dark walls warily. "We've been walking an awfully long time."

"It's fine," Ace said with a dismissive wave of his hand. "Hades is in the deepest part of the cave. Obviously."

Althea shrugged. "Whatever. I'm just saying, it's been a while. Like, a long while."

"The underworld isn't a mall, Althea," Ayla said with a scowl. "Obviously, it's pretty big."

"Obviously, it's pretty big," Althea mocked under her breath.

I sighed, feeling frustrated by Althea's questioning—and her sour disposition.

I didn't begrudge her anything—not her new goddess or her new owl. But her attitude—softly abrasive on a good day—seemed to have hardened sharply in the last hour since her visit from Hecate.

I looked down at Lothian.

You know, my other problem.

If Althea's discomfort appeared to grow, the exasperating wolf seemed to have grown somewhat comfortable with the situation. Wyatt, Norden and Larry had, too—at least as far as I could tell. They all scanned the darkness, ears up, glancing back every once in a while.

I reached down and grasped Lothian's fur to see if the telepathic link was still active. Instantly, I felt a kindling of connection with him—electric, as though a thousand tiny sparks had suddenly set my head alight.

He looked up at me in surprise.

Once again, Lothian's thoughts entered my mind. "You can hear what I'm thinking, can't you?" he asked, his mind's voice far more calm than it was before. "By the way, I can feel your anxiety even when you're not touching me. It's making me uneasy."

"I'd apologize, but to excuse myself I'll just point out we're wandering around hell," I thought at Lothian. "I think a little anxiousness is called for." I allowed myself to drift into the rushing stream of thoughts and images that flowed from Lothian's mind toward me. When he didn't answer, I asked, "Can you hear what I'm thinking?"

"I can." His large body shoved against me. "Be careful. You almost tripped."

"Thanks." I reoriented myself on the path and tried to find a happy medium between watching where I was going and psychically chatting with a wolf. I looked up. "Ami, can you hear me? Ami?" I turned my head toward Althea. "How about you, newly minted priestess of Hecate? You have any new tricks?" Nothing. "Ayla?" Three out of three sisters could not hear my mental speech. "I guess it's just you."

"Naw, it's not just the wolf," Archie grumbled.

"Yeah, but I already know you're nosy," I thought back.

"Astra?" Lothian interjected.

"Yes?"

"You're touching me," Lothian pointed out politely. His thoughts were hesitant, as if he wasn't sure if he should be speaking this way. "If you touch one of them, you might communicate telepathically with them, too."

"Um. Right." An unfamiliar tingling sensation spread through my body, filling me with a sense of embarrassment. "Thanks."

"Dolt," Archie muttered directly into my head.

"Shut up," I thought back.

"Sorry, what? Can't quite hear you."

* * *

AFTER A FEW SUBTLE experiments in telepathy as we walked, it was clear a few minutes later that

my powers hadn't changed in the underworld—
the connection between Lothian and I had. My
psychometry power had not morphed into full
blown two-way telepathy. It was my connection
with the wolf—and only that one wolf—that had
changed.

Even when I didn't touch him, a whisper of a
link seemed to remain between us. It was a
distant tingle that gave me a vague sense of what
Lothian was thinking and feeling. I could see a
flash of a thought or a feeling at times—but it was
only a flash.

The feeling was so faint, though, I wasn't sure
it wasn't all my imagination, or a trick of the
underworld.

When my hand was buried in his fur, I could
feel his fierce loyalty and his eagerness to keep
everyone safe in this strange situation we were in.
Lothian, the greedy, jerky, insulting man, was an
unexpected whirlwind of admirable emotions
and motivations as a wolf—

"Are you okay?" Ace asked me.

I blinked, realizing we'd reached a natural
barrier in the cave. "Yeah, I'm fine. I was just off
in my head."

"Are you sure?" he asked slowly, as if talking
to a child.

"I said I'm fine."

We'd arrived at a massive rock wall, at least thirty feet tall, with small stairways leading up and down to smaller hallways carved into the wall. The cavern we were in had grown dark, and the lantern Ace was holding was the only source of light. While I was stuck in my head, examining my newfound canine connection, all the torches that lined the walls had gone out or vanished..

Was it a power?

I mean—

Ugh. Focus, Astra.

The lantern flickered against the stone wall, casting eerie shadows over us. "Hades is in the deepest part of the cave, right?" I asked.

"Yep," Ace answered.

"So where do we go? Which one of these leads us to him? Probably not the ones that go up, right?" I asked. Though the stairways up could lead us out of this place. I glanced around at the six of us. Everyone stared back at me, waiting for me to choose the right direction. "Why are you all looking at me?"

Ace gave me an amused smile. "Don't worry. The choice isn't up to you." He patted my shoulder, and I wasn't sure if he was encouraging or mocking me. "It's Archie's second test."

Second test?

Archie shot him an annoyed look. "Second test?" the owl asked in surprise. "What do you mean, second test? No one's given me a test."

"Well, not that you recognized, no."

"What does that mean?" The owl fluttered his wings and leaned forward, looking between Ace and an increasingly smug-looking Lily resting on Althea's shoulder. "I didn't get any test at all. Do you think I wouldn't recognize—"

"Popcorn," Lily said.

Ace lifted his hands and hushed the second raptor. "Lily, that's not fair. You knew about that before it happened."

My eyes narrowed. Oh, she did, did she?

"I'm not showing off my knowledge, Ace," she told him sweetly. "I'm just rubbing in that he had no clue."

"Oh, for the love of Hecate," Althea stomped her foot and waved toward the small passages. "Who cares? It's over. Okay, he failed the first test. Okay. Is anyone here surprised? I mean, really?"

I closed my fist and felt myself vibrate with indignation. "Wait a minute—"

"No one said he failed the test." Ayla

interrupted as she glared at Althea. "Wow, you know something? You've turned into a real b—"

"Ayla!" Ami said sharply.

"I'm just saying what everyone here is thinking," Ayla muttered. "Let's just get this over with." She walked forward and pointed to a passageway off to the right, the dark steps descending even deeper into the rocky terrain. "I think it's that one. Anyone disagree?" When no one answered, she trudged up the first flight of stairs and stood before the descending hollow, pausing for a moment to look back at us. "Coming?"

Ace and Lily exchanged a look.

"Ayla, just hold up. Let's back up a minute." I turned away from the wall of hallways. "What test did Archie fail?" I asked Ace, who shook his head.

Ayla looked down at me. "Sorry. I'm just impatient."

"It's fine. But what does popcorn have to do—"

And then it hit me.

"It's okay, Ayla. It's been a long day. I ate little at the party, and even after the snack, I'm still hungry," Ami admitted. "It's making me a little punchy, too."

"The snack," I whispered.

"Probably more hungry than when you arrived," Lily said, her voice calm and deliberate. Almost gleeful. "And definitely more punchy."

Althea and Lily's laughter echoed like a buzz, their snickers like spikes digging into my ears. I turned toward Lily—and Althea—in a barely contained simmering fury. I was about two steps from punching that owl—and possibly Althea—in the face.

"Jeez, what?" my sister asked, her white owl still snickering, when she caught my expression.

"I get that you're going through something and life may have changed for you. I totally comprehend that this trip might feel like a jackpot win to you. I've had moments like that in my life, something good in a sea of bad. I understand better than you think—but never have I ever gotten amusement out of danger to any of you," I told Althea sternly. "If you are? I suggest you get yourself under control and stop showing it. Because you're making me angry."

Her face fell. "What the hell, Astra? Risk of danger to who?" Althea asked.

"Ami, of course," Lily explained helpfully.

I tasted the bile in my mouth, the acid burn of my stomach, a creeping sensation of dread as I realized how much more serious this situation had become.

Because of popcorn.

"Your sister ate the popcorn Ace presented to you all when you arrived, and no one bothered to explain to her that eating food in the underworld binds you to it."

"To what?" Ayla asked, but her face fell as she realized, too, exactly what had happened.

"To the underworld. I'm bound to the underworld. I can't leave," Ami whispered, her face white. Her eyes dropped, and she stared at Lothian in horror. "Oh, no! I gave the bag to Lothian when I was done with it."

I reached down slowly and filled my hand with his soft fur. With a defeated tone, the wolf admitted he'd eaten the rest. "It was good," he said by way of explanation. "Lots of butter."

"Archimedes could have told you all the situation to avoid. He could have informed you that eating anything in the underworld—even popcorn—would bind you to it," Ace said sympathetically. "He did not."

"It's a pretty brilliant form of manipulation, if you think about it," Althea murmured, contemplating Ami with concern. Then she bit her lip and glanced down at her feet.

Archie looked devastated.

Lothian looked furious.

* * *

"IT'S MY FAULT," Archie whispered.

"No, it's not," I blurted.

"I should have known. I should have stopped them."

We seemed to agree without saying anything that we would take a break in this dark cavern before Archie's second test.

The wolves moved just slightly to the right. I could see Wyatt and Norden nuzzling Lothian comfortingly as Lawrence stared suspiciously at Ace (who was talking to Althea and Lily.)

Ami sat on the stone floor, her face buried in her hands. Ayla sat next to her, her eyes wide with worry.

"It's not your fault, Archie," I breathed. "Someone offered us popcorn. Ami was hungry, and she took it. None of us blame you. We all had the same lessons about the Greek myths. Everyone here knew not to eat food in the underworld—including Ami. We will fix this. Together."

Archie noticed the uncertainty in my eyes as I spoke.

It was true. I was much more concerned than I had been moments before. I was worried we wouldn't be able to get out of here. That even if we did, Lothian and Ami might be trapped here indefinitely, like the other lost souls who haunted this place.

This was feeling like my fault.

Had I just been paying attention, had I just been more careful, if I didn't touch the obviously magical pedestal…none of us would be in this mess. We would be safe at home, or at least still in the human world where we belonged.

But because of me, we're stuck here in the underworld with no way out.

"We need to choose a path," Ayla said with a raised voice, her eyes on the ground. "There's no going back now. We can either keep going forward and hope that we find a way out, or we can turn around and go back the way we came hoping Ace is a lying sack of—"

"Ayla," Ami whispered dejectedly.

Ayla stopped herself and squeezed Ami's hand. "I think we need to decide quickly—I don't think any of us want to stay here any longer than we have to. I think the longer we're here, the more chance there is for us all to make mistakes."

I nodded, my throat tight.

She was right—we needed to choose a path. But which one? Ahead of us lay who knows what dangers, while behind us…well, at least we knew what was behind us.

I looked at my owl. "Archie?"

"No," Ayla said shortly. She scrambled up off the floor and pointed toward the pathway she chose previously. "That one leads to Hades, and he's the only one that can let Lothian and Ami go," she said with conviction. She glanced at me. "I think you were right. I don't think this is about Archie. Well, not only about him." Ayla looked at me, her eyes full of hope. "I think this is about us."

Althea nodded. "If that's true, then we have to have each other's backs." She turned and faced the stairs Ayla had chosen. "I'm with you," she said. "You're the only death speaker here. You'd know which way Hades was. I mean, if anyone would."

"I guess—" Ami said in a soft voice. She looked up at Ayla. "I guess I'm with you, too."

Archie took a deep breath. He looked from Ami to Ayla and then to me. "But Ace said this was my test. If she chooses and I don't, do I fail?"

"I can't tell you that," Ace responded.

"Some tour guide you are," Ayla muttered. "Look, Archie, I can't tell you what to do here. What I can tell you, though, is these idiots already changed the rules they claimed we were supposed to abide by with the popcorn. That toy soldier said he would tell you the tests and whether you pass or fail. He lied." Archie thought back, and then nodded. "I'm telling you. I know where Hades is. He's down that hallway." She pointed emphatically. "I promise."

"Okay," Archie nodded once more. "I'm with you, too."

As if on cue, the wind blew a small breeze over the wall, and the cave was plunged into darkness.

"Oh, come on!" Ayla shouted.

There was no way to see which path we needed to take.

CHAPTER NINE

"Quiet!" Ami hissed. "Listen."

The subtle, echoing sigh reached up from the depths of the abyss, causing the very air to tremble in its wake. To anyone else, it would have passed unnoticed or been dismissed as wind whistling through the caves.

"What is it?" Althea asked.

"Well, you're now priestessed to a witch goddess. Can't you blink, wiggle your nose, and tell us?" Ayla asked sarcastically.

I could practically feel Ayla's gaze, like the heat from a sniper's sight, seeking the slightest flaw in Althea's defenses.

"Stop it, both of you. This feels... wrong."

"What do you mean, wrong?" Althea asked.

"I don't know," Ami replied. "It just feels like something bad is about to happen."

As if in response to her words, the sound increased in intensity, becoming a throaty rumble that seemed to shake the very ground we were standing on.

"Oh great," I said, trying not to fidget. "Now what?"

"What the hell is that?" Althea exclaimed.

"It's the dark," Archie said simply.

"But what is it?" she pressed, her voice shaking.

"He told you. It's just the dark," Ayla said, her voice laced with smug arrogance. "There's nothing to be afraid of."

"I can see," Archie said.

"As can I," Lily added. "We're fine."

"Of course we're fine. I may not see like the owls, I'm not scared of the dark like some child," Ayla said.

Lothian and Wyatt barked one after another.

My eyes narrowed into slits as I tried to look around me, but it was pitch black in this cave. I could see nothing, which meant I couldn't tell if there was anything around us. I knew that the noise seemed to be getting louder.

"Why are we sitting here doing nothing?" Ayla

asked. "The birds and the wolves can see. I have no doubt one of them remembers which cave hole I pointed to." I heard her footsteps to my right. "We have four wolves. Two owls. That's six creatures that are perfectly at home in the dark."

"Just hold on. Does anyone have matches or a lighter?" I asked. "We're witches. We do candle magic. Surely someone has something that would make a flame."

"You didn't bring one of your fancy stolen military light rock things?" Ayla asked—now from my left.

"I don't wander around our house carrying weapons, no."

"That's not a weapon. It's a magic flashlight." I heard fabric being rifled through. "You really have nothing on you?"

"What kind of person do you think I am?" Far off, I heard the soft sound of snorting and slobbering. "Matches? Lighter? No one?"

Ayla sighed. "I think you're the kind of person who would have been a lot more useful if you'd thought to bring a flashlight."

As I was about to give Ayla a piece of my mind, she spit out, "Got it." Her obnoxious tone made me lose my train of thought, and before I could ask her what she had, she struck a match.

"Nice," Ami murmured.

"Apparently, I can still psychically yank stuff from my room through the ether." The light from the match illuminated Ayla's face for a moment before she cupped her hand around it and brought it close to her chest. In the brief light, I saw her eyes were wide and her skin was pale—her arrogant tone wasn't a return to the "old Ayla." It was a cover for her fear. "Did anyone else hear that besides me?"

I raised an eyebrow. "The slobbering?"

She nodded. "I guess you heard it."

"What is it?" Ami asked, her voice little more than a whisper.

"I don't know," Ayla replied. "But whatever it is, I think it's coming closer."

Ayla's words hung in the air for a moment before being drowned out by a sinister growl. I turned toward it, and my heart stopped. It came from behind us.

And it was definitely louder.

That meant it was getting closer.

Suddenly, there was a red glow.

Mist curled and drifted up from the ground. Whatever owned those glowing red embers floating in the darkness was all but obscured by the fog. I heard the deep and guttural sounds of a fearsome beast. Maybe multiple fearsome beasts—

—that stopped, tilted its heads, and barked happily.

With a mighty leap, Cerberus landed in front of us, his powerful jaws snapping as his glowing eyes helpfully lighting up the cave we were in and dwarfing Ayla's puny match light. He wagged his tail eagerly and let out a low growl.

"Good dog," Ayla told him affectionately while putting out the match. "You're like Rudolph the Red-Nosed Reindeer."

"Only more murderous," Ami said.

Cerberus snorted and looked down at us quizzically. He placed a cold wet nose on my forehead, and then he licked my hand. "What is it?" I asked him.

Cerberus snarled again and lowered his bulk, indicating that I should mount his back. The number-three head turned toward me, his eyes tinged yellow-red, and then he flicked a tongue the size of a tire iron. Tucked into the collar of the hell hound were several thin, short torches.

I loosened them and held them up.

"Nice!" Althea said.

"Oh, crap," Ayla said. The match she had extinguished was still in her hand. "Maybe I shouldn't have snuffed out that match. I'm not sure where the other ones are in my room, and I have to picture them to teleport them here."

The gigantic hell hound presented the left-most head.

And there were the matches.

"Well, you're definitely prepared, aren't you?" I said, grabbing the matches.

The giant three-headed dog wagged his tail happily and barked.

"He's a sweetheart," Ayla replied, rubbing the dog behind one ear and then the other.

Ami sniffled and brushed the hair out of her eyes. "Well, good, maybe he'll share his den with Lothian and I since the two of us will be stuck here for an eternity," she said. "We'll need somewhere to sleep, and he seems soft."

"That's assuming you're not thrown in a pit somewhere," Ayla pointed out. "If you have to stay here, I doubt they'll just let you wander around and build a life here."

Ami stared at Ayla in shock, and then quietly began to sob, her face in her hands.

"Jeez, Ayla, what is wrong with you?" Althea hissed.

"I mean, I could be wrong!" Ayla said quickly.

Althea and I put our arms around Ami,

comforting her. Ami sobbed harder, and I watched as her shoulders shook with the force of her tears.

Great.

* * *

"I'm so sorry," Ayla said, putting out her hand to comfort our sobbing sister.

Ami sobbed and shook her head.

"Ami, come on. I'm so sorry," Ayla repeated. "I just don't think before I talk sometimes. You know that. We will not let you get stuck down here. No way."

Ami sniffled and wiped her nose on the sleeve of her shirt. "I know. I know you didn't mean to hurt my feelings," she said. "I just can't believe after all that studying, all those years of Mom's lectures, and getting A's on my underworld test, I just up and ate that stupid popcorn. I'm embarrassed that I didn't think twice."

"Come on, Ami," I said. "Everyone makes mistakes."

She looked up at me with red eyes. "Sometimes I just feel you're all so much smarter than me. Althea can do potions, and Ayla can talk to the dead and teleport things across the spirit realm, and Astra, you're like a witchy James Bond—"

"Yeah, I'm definitely not," I told her, shaking my head in the red light of Cerberus's glowing eyes. "We all have our strengths and weaknesses." I lit a torch from Cerberus's collar and a brighter, more cheerful light washed over the cavern.

I mean, sort of.

It was as cheerful a light as we could get in hell.

"I get why you feel overwhelmed. But we just need to follow the plan and keep moving," I continued. "Ayla picked the passageway. We all agreed that's the way we need to go. Hades' guard dog seems to be helping us and not stopping us. All in all," I told her with a smile, "things could go a lot worse."

She gave a half-smile and dabbed her watery eyes with the cuff of her plain white shirt. I could feel the clammy sweat on her neck as she sniffled, trying to gain control. It was heartbreaking to see her break like this.

"I think that sounds like a good idea," she said finally, taking a deep breath. "I'm ready. We can start moving through the passageway as soon as everyone is ready to go."

"Good deal. And don't worry. We'll figure

something out," I said, giving Ami one last squeeze. "We always do. We will not leave you here alone. We'll get through Hades together, and we'll escape hell."

Ami nodded slowly, her puffy face streaked with tears.

I glanced up from comforting Ami and saw Ayla with a look of surprise and fear on her face. The light from the small torch spilled around her in an odd halo effect, even as the rest of the room was cloaked in darkness.

"What is it?" I asked.

"I think... I think we have a problem," Ayla said slowly.

"What kind of problem?" Althea asked.

One hand covered her mouth as she withdrew back into the jagged rock wall. "We may have gained a Cerberus in the darkness, but we also lost an Ace. Ace is gone," Ayla said.

"Surely not." The color drained from Ami's face as she looked around and confirmed for herself what Ayla was saying. "But how? Where did he go?"

I didn't care.

I wasn't sure, at this point, the ground under my feet could be trusted.

"Who cares?" I asked in a way that made it

clear it wasn't a question. "In case anyone forgot, he was the one who gave Ami the bag of popcorn. I was fine following him because we didn't have many options, but let's be honest—there was no sign we should trust the guy completely, right?"

"Look, I'm not saying he should or shouldn't be trusted, but I am getting hungry." Althea grunted as she shifted Lily from one arm to the other. "I'm sure the wolves are getting hungry, too. We've been in this place too long already."

"Sorry, are you in charge now?" Ayla asked. "I get that you just got a new goddess and a pet totally inappropriate to the climate in Florida, but that doesn't make you queen for a day."

"Well, I don't see you coming up with any plans," Althea replied. "You just pointed to a hole in the wall."

The sisters glared at each other, neither willing to give up ground. I felt like I was in the middle of an intense game of Risk, and these two were about to go to war.

In the silence, my stomach growled.

The humidity from the cave reminded me of the steamed dumplings I had consumed just hours earlier. I pushed the tasty memory from my mind, trying to ignore my grumbling tummy and focus on the task at hand.

Ami drew her face into a mild frown. "So this is you saying…what? Do you have a point, or are you two just going to be nasty to each other?"

"I'm saying that we can't sit here in this room forever." Althea's eyebrow rose. "I'm not saying we should go and not worry about the guy who gave Ami a bag of popcorn. But he lives here. I'm sure he's fine. I'm just saying we should move on. We won't make progress standing here doing nothing."

"So, you're basically saying what Astra said," Ayla said with scorn. "Again."

"No, she's agreeing, Ayla," I said. "And to be honest, it's not like we have any way to contact Ace and ask him what happened, anyway," I added.

"Fine, let's move forward."

"We're all in agreement, then?" Ami asked.

"Yes. You know, I said that at the start of this whole thing, so I don't know how Althea can 'come up' with that idea," Ayla grumbled. She sighed again and rubbed Cerberus behind his head. "Sorry, bro. I know you're just looking out for us." With a pained expression, she continued: "We have to move on now, right? I know you won't fit through that doorway."

All three heads whined, but they followed as

we moved up the stairway. Cerberus seemed to get smaller as we climbed, until he was nothing more than a large black dog at our heels, slightly smaller than the wolves glued to our sides.

Well.

A black dog with three heads.

Cerberus's six eyes glowed a bright green in the darkness. His fur was still as thick, and his three heads were still alert and watchful, but he seemed less imposing now.

I chuckled. "I guess we really did trade Ace for Cerberus."

The stairway seemed to go on forever.

I lost count of how many times we turned, rose, and descended. Every time the stairway changed directions, the darkness shifted slightly. I had the distinct feeling that something was watching us, but whenever I tried to look back, there was nothing there.

I kept my hand on the wall, feeling my way in the dimly lit stairwell as we progressed. I tried not to think about how deep down we were or how long it would take to get back if we had to turn around. How everyone was getting stressed out, so stressed that they were attacking each other.

Stop it, Astra.

Concentrate on each step. One step at a time. Just go forward.

Lothian's claws clicked on the stone steps as he walked close to my side. His body brushed against mine, his colossal head a little above my hip. I could feel his heat, and it was strangely comforting in the firelight. Sometimes I would feel his wet nose lightly touch the back of my arm and I flinched in surprise, but was never scared.

Finally, Ayla held up a hand, and we all stopped. "I hear something," she whispered. "It's up ahead." She pointed, and we moved toward an opening. The path ahead stretched out before us, lit by an eerily bright orange-yellow light.

"What is that?" Althea asked, squinting into the distance.

"I don't know, but I think we should be careful," Ayla said.

Thick clouds of mist obscured the way forward, and Ayla shivered as if she felt a chill. She stepped back and tucked herself between me and Ami.

"What's wrong?" Althea asked, her eyes on the horizon.

Ayla didn't answer, but glanced at Cerberus. The dog stood tall and straight, ears forward and alert. He glanced back at Ayla for a moment, then whined while shifting restlessly.

"I think… I think we should go back," Ayla said slowly.

"Why? What's wrong?" I asked.

Ayla shook her head. "I don't know. But something doesn't feel right. And Cerberus is getting really agitated."

I looked at the hell hound.

Cerberus whined again and pawed at the ground. He looked up at Ayla with his six glowing eyes, and she stroked his head gently. With a huff, Cerberus let out a low growl, then bounded away toward the mist. Then he came back and leaned against Ayla's leg heavily.

"Ayla, I think he wants you to follow him," Althea said.

Cerberus whined again and backed up.

"No, no, let's go back," Ayla said quickly. "We can find another way. There has to be another way."

"What? No! We can't turn back now!" Althea protested.

Ayla tensed up beside me, and I put a hand on her arm. "It's okay," I breathed. "We don't have to go any closer if you don't want to. At least not at this very moment."

"Then what do we do, stand here and do nothing?" Althea asked me, an edge to her voice.

"We find out what's bothering Ayla and deal with it," I told Althea harshly.

Something was bothering Ayla, but she refused to tell us what it was. Cerberus had also returned to her side and was now standing protectively in front of her. Ami and I exchanged a worried look, but neither of us said anything.

Ayla was quiet for a moment, then she sighed. "I'm sorry," she mumbled. "It's just... this place feels really off to me. Like something bad is going to happen."

"What do you think is causing that feeling?" I asked her gently.

Ayla shook her head. "I don't know. It's just a feeling I have."

She shook her head and wrapped her arms around herself. "I don't know. But I have a terrible feeling about this."

"Okay," I said slowly. "Let's go back then."

Althea opened her mouth to protest, but I shot her a warning look as Cerberus let out a howl of protest.

The four of us—well, eight if you count the wolves, ten if you added the birds—turned as one to look at the hell hound. He was staring longingly into the mist like it was made of beef jerky, his body tense and quivering. A low growl escaped his throat, and his hackles were raised as he glanced back at Ayla.

Althea looked at Ayla. "Ayla, he wants you to follow him."

"Do you trust the hell hound, or your gut?" Ami asked.

Ayla shook her head, her eyes scanning the mist carefully. "I don't know," she said softly. All her usual bravado was gone, replaced by a fear that she didn't seem to fully understand. "But he really wants me to go into that stuff, huh?"

The hell hound barked as if to answer her.

Ayla glanced away guiltily. "It's probably nothing," she murmured. "I'm just being paranoid."

We all stood there for a moment, waiting and listening carefully. But all we could hear was the sound of our own breathing and the rustle of clawed paws on the stone.

My youngest sister's keen eyes were focused on a single, faraway point somewhere within the mist. Finally, she seemed to swallow her fear and said, "Okay. I think we should keep going."

So we did.

CHAPTER TEN

The heat hit me like a furnace blast, and my shirt grew wet with perspiration. Sweat slid down my face, tickling like some kind of soft insect.

Ugh.

We'd been trapped in a white noise vacuum, with only cave sounds, water, fire, and the occasional gust of wind to break the silence of the underworld. Now there were screams, laughter, and tears just out of our view.

No, not screams…shrieks?

Was that laughter?

"People laugh in hell?" Ami asked, surprised.

"You heard a laugh, too?"

She nodded.

"What is this place?" I murmured, taking in my surroundings. "Is it real, or—"

Althea snorted. "So, Astra, when you say real, what, precisely, do you mean by real?"

She had a point.

Cerberus whined and pressed closer to Ayla's side, gently propelling her forward. It was an encouragement that alarmed the wolves— Lothian growled loudly in response, trying to ward him off. But Cerberus was persistent.

"What's wrong with your hell hound?" Ami asked, eyeing the animals warily. "If he doesn't quit, one of those wolves is going to take a bite out of his hindquarters."

Ayla glared. "How did he become my hell hound?"

Althea rolled her eyes. "Oh, come on. He's clearly attached to you."

The wolves stared at each other for a long moment, their tails swishing in unison as they thought about what to do next. Finally, with an almost imperceptible nod from Ayla, Lothian walked forward and touched his nose to one of Cerberus's three heads.

The creature's eyes widened, and he let out a low, rumbling growl.

Lothian huffed.

Cerberus seemed to relax, taking a deep breath and releasing it slowly, and once released, Lothian huffed once more and returned to my side.

I had no idea what on earth just transpired.

I wrapped an arm around Lothian's neck and dropped to his level, feeling his soft fur. "Well?" I asked him silently. "What was that about?"

"He doesn't mean us any harm. I mean, we're dogs. We don't lie, Astra. I'm not sure that we can, really. Not in this form." That was an interesting tidbit I never knew before, and not one I was sure I believed. "He doesn't want anything to happen to any of us, but he thinks we should move toward that ridge and look."

I glanced up and saw what looked more like a cliff than a ridge. "What do you think?"

"I think we have no choice but to keep going."

Right.

With a swish of his crooked tail, Cerberus led us to the edge of the ravine. We huddled close together, our hearts hammering in our chests, gazing down at the maelstrom we expected to find below.

I blinked.

Wait.

What the heck?

It was a street—a blue-canopied shopping center from a time gone by where alleys and kiosks were filled with merchandise from... somewhere. There was an odd air of festivity, as if it were a carnival—merry merchants laughing and gossiping as they surveyed their wares. White flowers draped over every corner, sign, and booth, while white petals drifted down to the ground like a gentle rain blanketing the streets in perfumed, floral snow.

How did flowers even grow here?

I looked up.

Yep. Top of a cave.

I looked back down, confused.

Whatever this place was, it looked to be vibrant and...alive. There was no other way to describe it.

There were crowds of people moving in all directions as they went about their business. Some appeared to argue over prices or pointed excitedly at some new discovery; others laughed and drank from steins of ale or wine; and still others danced wildly to a nearby live band.

They looked like they were just living their lives.

But they couldn't be alive.

This was the underworld.

"They're dead. I mean, they all must be dead," Ayla said, doubt quivering her voice. She flicked her hand toward Althea. "You can see them too, right? I'm not seeing a town of ghosts none of you can see?"

"Yep, I can see them all," she admitted.

Ami and I acknowledged we could see the town as well.

There were fauns, pixies, and elves—people from every different kind of mortal life imaginable, actually. There were also many, many humans.

"We are definitely not in Florida anymore," I muttered, sniffing the air.

"No, we're definitely not," Althea said, her eyebrow cocked and her expression deadpan. "But at least we're not in that other place anymore."

"What other place?" Ami asked.

"You know, the place where everything is shrouded in shadow and you can't tell what's going on. The place we just left." Althea shook her head. "It was the worst place I've ever seen. Or not seen, to be more accurate." She smiled at her snowy owl. "Though Hecate was cool."

"So, the other end of that hall, you mean?" Ayla pointed behind us. "It wasn't even that dark.

And I think we're still there, anyway. So don't get too excited."

We walked down a path leading to the town.

Ayla's complexion grew rosier and rosier as we closed in. The sound of drums reverberated through me, making the blood pound in my veins. "Everybody okay?" I asked.

My sisters all responded they were fine.

A shady looking character stopped us before we even made it halfway to the gate. He had stringy, shoulder length hair and a dark, wispy beard. "You there! Hey, you gotta pay the toll," he said with a grin.

The drums abruptly stopped.

"What?" Ayla exclaimed, her eyes growing wide.

"A toll?" I asked. "What's this all about?"

The man shrugged. "Just the way things are. Everyone works to keep the city running. We do what we do because we have to. There is nothing sinister here, and no reason to fear," he continued, his eyes narrowing, "unless you have something to hide, or can't afford to pay the toll."

"Do you have a ferry?" Ayla asked, wondering if the man that greeted us was Charon, the ferryman of Hades that helps the dead by ferrying the newly deceased across the Acheron and Styx rivers to the afterlife.

"He's my boss, and that's a gate," he said, pointing. "Not a river. Don't get paranoid."

Ayla eyed the man like a snake weighing its curiosity, but as none of us moved or said a word, she said, "Fine. We'll pay." She dug into her pockets and pulled out a handful of coins. "Is this enough?"

The man scooped up the quarters and made grabby-hands for the nickels, but he seemed afraid to touch the pennies. "They'll bring me good luck," he said, winking. "Those copper coins will just upset the queen."

"The queen?" I asked. "Who's the queen?"

But he ignored me.

The bearded man finished counting the coins from Ayla. He nodded to her. "This is more than enough for you all to enter—though it's not enough to buy you dinner and a limo to the prom," he said, pocketing the coins. "So, yeah. Cool."

"Cool?" Ayla asked.

"Yep. Cool. Cool, cool, cool. And welcome," he said, extending his hand in a manner that most would consider old-fashioned, "to Asphodel Meadows."

* * *

NONE OF MY TEACHERS—MY mother, or those at the academy—spent a lot of time talking about Asphodel Meadows. That was understandable, since there wasn't a lot known about it.

The Asphodel Meadows is the afterlife for people who have done neither good nor bad things in their lives.

There.

That's what I know.

"This is that mediocre place, right?" Althea asked. "Where the mediocre people go after they die?"

Several people walking by glanced with annoyance at my sister. "Just ignore her," one of their party said. "We need to make sure we get to the bar in time to hear that new fusion hardcore trance dubstep rap rock band."

The townspeople walked down the dirt road, lips curled in distaste. Their scrawny, floofy dog yipped at the wolves as they passed.

"Heroes journey to the Fields of Elysium. It's said that the less heroic people, the ones who just lived their lives quietly without making waves, come to Asphodel Meadows," Ami corrected Althea. She leaned against the stall closest to us, her arms crossed in front of her. "Maybe I should find a real estate agent. You think there are any condos here?" She cast a downward glance at Lothian. "At least it appears they allow pets."

"It could be worse," Althea said, a smirk on her face. "This could be Tartarus."

Lily bobbed her white head in agreement.

"You know, you two owls are being awfully quiet," I said, glancing at Lily on Althea's shoulder and turning to pay special attention to Archie. "You guys usually chime in with your two cents' worth, but you've been remarkably unhelpful throughout this little hike."

"So?" said Lily from my sister's shoulder.

"So just what I said," I told Lily while still focusing all my attention on Archie. "It seems you two have been keeping quiet. That's unlike you, so I suspect it's unlike her. Nothing to say about Asphodel Meadows?"

Archie blinked his large, yellow eyes at me. "What would you like us to say about Asphodel Meadows, mistress?"

"Wow," I deadpanned. "So it's like that now, is it?"

Archie stared at me with an impudent stare and then he gave an indignant hoot of dismissive protest.

"What on earth was that?" I asked, leaning in closer.

"That?" Archie whispered in a low, conspiratorial voice. "That's the sound an owl makes when it's"—he leaned forward, his beak close to my ear—"STARVING!"

He leaped off my arm as I winced back. "Ow."

"What?" Althea asked, looking at me.

I shook my head. "Nothing. Just an owl hooting in my ear."

Althea snorted and turned back to Ami.

I turned back to Archie, who was now perched on top of a nearby stall, his eyes closed and head nodding as if he was about to take a nap.

"Hey!" I called up to him. "No sleeping on the job! I get that you're hungry. So are we. But we can't have anyone else ingesting anything grown here in the underworld. And these are supposed to be your tests, dude. Maybe you wanna stay awake?"

Archie cracked one eye open and looked down at me. "Yes, mistress," he said with a yawn, before closing his eye again.

I rolled my eyes and shook my head. This place would be the death of me. But at least it wasn't technically the Tartarus part of the underworld. I would take Asphodel Meadows any day, no matter how mediocre it may be.

"Oh, come on," Althea said with a roll of her eyes to something Ami said. "Nothing about Asphodel Meadows is all that exciting. It's just a bunch of dead people wandering around aimlessly. How much more bland could it get?"

"Bland is fine. Bland might be less dangerous," I told her. "And remember, Cerberus wanted Ayla to check this place out."

"So, we're following the three-headed dog now?"

"He is supposed to be the guardian of Hades."

"Yeah, I think you're getting your mythological dudes mixed up." Ami and Ayla stopped and turned toward Althea. "Cerberus's job is to prevent the dead from leaving. Not guard Hades." She looked down at the triple-headed dog. "For all we know, he's sticking with us to make sure we don't leave."

"Or," Ayla said with a frown, "he's decided to show us where Hercules took him out of the underworld. You don't know."

We all stared at the dog blankly. He whined softly and laid down.

Althea looked at me. "Read him."

I looked at her. "Althea, no. I am not reading

an underworld hell hound." I'll admit I wasn't always the first person to remember I had powers, much less to use them, but there was no way in hell I was reading anything that lived in hell.

"Yes. Yes, you are," she said. "Read him."

"No. You're out of your mind," I said.

"There's no need for that! It's vague, but I remember someone gave Cerberus to Hercules. Remember?" Ayla said, her eyes darting between Althea, Ami, and me. "They put him in adamant chains and then Herc drug Cerberus out of the underworld after fighting with him. Or something."

We stared back blankly.

"Not ringing a bell?"

We shook our heads.

"You know, all that stuff Mom tried to teach us about the Greek myths probably would have been good to pay attention to." Ayla crossed her arms. "The long and the short of it? That dog knows the way out."

Cerberus stood at attention proudly and panted.

"Even if that's true," I pointed out, "we don't know if we can leave. We don't know why we're here, who brought us here, and what we're supposed to do."

"And I don't think I can just walk out," Ami added quietly.

"We're going in circles." Ayla turned around and walked a few feet away. I could see her shoulders moving up and down as she breathed deeply. Finally, she turned back. "Look, I get it—we don't know why we're here, we're not getting information, and the one dude that was telling us anything disappeared. But all we're doing is getting led around by the nose, and we're not finding anything out."

"That's not entirely true. Althea got an owl and a new goddess. Maybe that's why we're here."

Ami took a deep breath and pulled the glowing star card from her pocket. "This is still glowing. Archie's still in danger."

Ayla's eyes widened, like she was about to tell us her deepest, darkest secret.

And then my youngest sister exploded.

* * *

"ALTHEA JUST LEFT Mom's coven! Just left! Oathed to another god without thinking!" Ayla shouted.

I frowned. "Ayla, calm down."

"I don't know that I'd put it that way, anyway,"

Althea said, her cheeks tinging a darker shade of red, her gaze dropping to the floor. "I'd been thinking about it for a while and—"

"We're all walking around here like we're afraid we're going to offend Athena if we step wrong!" Ayla's voice was rising with every word, and she cast wild, desperate looks around the group. "I mean, really? Are we just going to keep sitting on our hands while we get draggged around like this is a queue at Disney World?" Ayla's fists were clenched at her sides.

"I hope you're not saying that we should walk around recklessly or take unnecessary risks, Ayla," I drawled.

"Right, military witch—suddenly, you wanna be careful?"

Ouch.

"We need to stop this nonsense," she continued. "It's time for us to stop being so cautious and start taking some risks. We need to find Hades, figure out why we're down here, and get back home as quickly as possible. Otherwise, we may never return to our lives again."

"Look, I get it. I get your impatience," I said, "But this isn't anything I've dealt with before."

"Oh, for goodness—" Ayla took a deep breath, letting her anger and frustration subside for a moment. Then she turned toward me with a fierce look in her eyes. "Holy underworld goddesses, Astra. You and Archie aren't the only capable people here!"

"Hey! That's not fair. I never said we were," I retorted.

"Maybe not with words, but it's pretty clear you think it! You two always act like you know better than anyone else. But news flash—you don't! And neither do I! You think you're the only ones that can handle this because you have some kind of military training! But news flash: the rest of us are just as capable as you are—maybe even more so!"

Well.

I wouldn't go that far.

"We just need to take some risks and stop being afraid of what might happen."

That was a lot of news flashes.

"I know that." I leaned down to plant a quick kiss on Ayla's head, my hands gently massaging her fear-pinched shoulders. I smiled and spoke softly, trying to diffuse her eruption. "But you need to understand that I'm trying to be careful. We all are. This place is dangerous, and we have no idea what we're doing. So, please, can you bring it down a notch?"

She was silent for a long moment, her eyes boring into mine. Finally, she sighed and nodded. "Okay, fine. But we need to come up with a plan soon. We can't just keep wandering around down here."

I said nothing in response, not in public, but despite Ayla's anger?

We weren't just wandering around.

We'd been led to this place—first by the toy soldier, then by Ace, and now Cerberus. It was possible all those people showing up were just coincidences, but it was also possible this was someone's carefully constructed plan. The safest course of action was to follow that plan and try to understand it.

After all, this was the underworld. One false step and the shadow of death would envelop us all.

That, and if someone wanted us dead?

We'd be dead already.

Suddenly, a voice—ridiculously masculine in its tone and confident in its authority—interrupted my thoughts. "Excuse me, ladies."

I glanced up.

An Adonis stood a few scant meters away from us. He was stunningly handsome, with a wavy raven black mass of hair cascading over his broadly muscled shoulders. His piercing eyes were oddly colored with bright greens and blues, mottled in swirling patterns, like the sea.

"Can I help you?" I asked as I stepped in front of my sisters, my hand moving behind my back in case I needed to zap this bad boy with some surprise lightning.

Lothian then stepped in front of me.

"I couldn't help but overhear your conversation," he said. "And I have to say, I agree with the young lady. You can't just keep wandering around down here. It's not safe."

Ayla inched closer to me, her voice laced with venom. "It's not, huh?" Her eyes narrowed to slits. "Who are you?" she demanded.

He smiled briefly, as if amused by her moxie. The man then held up his hands in an appeasing gesture, but the impact of his next words froze us in place. "My name is Hades, and I rule this place."

CHAPTER ELEVEN

I stared at the man in front of me, trying to process the information.

Hades.

The Greek god of the underworld.

The ruler of the dead.

I know we were looking for him but…

Yeah.

I gulped.

"I'm here to help you," he said, his expression serious. "I'm not here to kill you."

Uh huh.

Good to know.

While the rest of us stared in surprise, Ayla narrowed her eyes at the god. "Why would you help us? We're strangers."

Hades had a distant look on his face, as if he were thinking. "Are you?" he murmured.

I couldn't help but notice Hades stared at Ayla like she was the most fascinating thing in the world, and she seemed to study him just as closely. It was like they were each trying to get a sense of the other's motives.

"Yes?" Ayla answered, her eyebrows arched and lips pursed. When she spoke, her voice dripped with incredulousness.

Ami looked nervously at our youngest sister.

"It's not every day four lovely ladies find their way into my realm, and it's even more rare for them to be accompanied by my hell hound." Hades paused, his eyes flicking toward the still-sniffing Cerberus. "I'm surprised he let you get this far without calling for me."

Cerberus barked.

The other two heads barked as well.

The dog sat on its hind legs, its tongues hanging out as it panted happily. I could've sworn it was smiling at Ayla. Hades' gaze turned from the dog to her, his expression serious.

He seemed...friendly," she said cautiously, as if she wasn't sure that was the right word, and then shifted uncomfortably under his gaze.

Hades barked out a laugh. "Friendly? No, my

dear, Cerberus is many things—loyal, fierce, protective—but he is not friendly," he intoned, his eyes fixed on Ayla's face. Hades stepped forward and reached out to pet one of the dog's heads, and Cerberus leaned into his master's touch with an almost contented sigh.

As this unexpected meeting progressed, I felt an odd sense of... kinship with Hades. It grew slowly, so slowly I barely noticed it. He seemed so powerful, yet he had a softness in his eyes as he looked at Ayla that belied his intimidating reputation.

Momentary relief flickered across Ayla's face but it quickly vanished. "He seems to like you," Ayla said cautiously.

"Like? I don't know about that, really. There are few that like me—"

"Wow. That's sad."

Hades looked at Ayla as if baffled by her response.

"That there aren't many people that like you. I would bet you're wrong about that, though," she told him with a tilt of her head.

"You're most likely right, young lady. My realm is... well, let's just say there are many people who are less than fond of me. Cerberus is loyal to me," Hades said, dropping his hand.

"More loyal than most that serve me." He cleared his throat and turned away, but something flickered in his eyes. "Let's move along. In the world above, you are the sister that can speak to the dead?"

Ayla stared at him, speechless.

"Yes," I said, a hint of suspicion in my voice. "She is."

"Astra!"

"Is it ever a good idea to lie to a god?" I asked Ayla.

"Ah, yes. Astra," Hades said, turning to look at me. "I sensed your power from the moment you stepped into my realm. You are the one that swallowed the beloved Star Maiden's power, the last of us to live among mortals."

Why couldn't gods just talk like normal people?

"I am—though last Christmas, I spent some time at Hermes's house. He was right in the middle of mortals in Palm Beach, along with—"

Hades held up his hand, and I stopped talking abruptly.

"You speak of different ages." He stepped closer and I fought the urge to step back. There was something about his presence that was both intoxicating and dangerous. "I don't want to hear about your time with the god of thieves or any other mortal antics you've been up to. What I want to know is why you're here, in my realm."

Ayla stepped forward, her expression earnest. "We were transported here by a toy soldier. The toy said that Archie"—my sister pointed to my owl—"needed to be tested, and then Ami"—Ayla pointed to Ami—"got a glowing star card that said Archie was in danger and then Astra grabbed the pedestal and we all wound up here." She looked next to her. "Like, instantly. Even the werewolves."

Hades frowned. "That sounds like quite a story," he said slowly, his eyes never leaving Ayla's face. "And you say this 'toy soldier' just transported you here with no warning?"

Ayla nodded. "Yes, that's right."

The god of the underworld paused for a moment and looked up as if lost in thought. After a few moments, he looked at me and then to the rest of my family (who were all watching the scene before them with various levels of confusion, surprise, and fear.) "I see," he said finally. "Well, it seems you've stumbled into my realm quite by accident, then."

"I know," Ayla said with a nod, her eyes not

leaving Hades for a second. "That's what I told you."

Slowly, a smile spread across Hades' face as he looked at Ayla. He seemed almost amused by the situation suddenly, as if this was all some strange game that had taken an unexpected turn.

"I don't like that look," Archie said fearfully.

Althea leaned in toward me. "Why does he keep looking at Ayla like that?" she whispered.

Hades stepped forward and placed his hand on Ayla's shoulder, gazing intently into her eyes. She seemed spellbound by his presence, unable to look away from him even for a second.

"Come," he breathed.

The god then turned and walked through the merchant stalls of the underworld marketplace. Althea and I exchanged looks, but before we could speak, Ayla took off after him without hesitation. Her right hand clutched Norden Morris's fur as the wolf hurried to keep up with her.

After a short walk through Asphodel Meadows, Hades came to a halt in front of a towering gate made of a glowing silvery metal. The stone walls on either side of the gate appeared to be carved limestone, and the rock glowed with an eerie reddish-yellow light that seemed to emanate from within the stone itself.

"What is this?" Ayla demanded.

"Welcome," he said as he gestured for us to follow him through the gate. "This is Netherworld Palace—my home."

* * *

I WAS awe-struck as I stepped through the gates of Netherworld Palace, entranced by its otherworldly beauty. Every inch of the palace was lavishly decorated with intricate carvings and gleaming silver accents, all shimmering like glittering jewels in the darkness of Hades' realm.

"Be careful," Hades pointed.

At the center of the palace's front walkway stood a gigantic black hole that dropped even deeper into the earth. It glittered with thousands upon thousands of tiny lights far below, tiny lights that were strong enough to illuminate the front of the palace in an ethereal light.

The smell of sulfur and brimstone gripped my nostrils tight as the hole's frightening depth stared back at me.

"You don't have to tell me twice," Althea said as she crept carefully around it.

I could feel an intense energy radiating from within the palace as we stepped beyond the hole, as if the very air itself had been imbued with power and magic. It was unlike anything I'd ever felt before, making my heart race and my breathing quicken.

Hades led us down endless corridors, each more opulent than the one before it. We passed glittering fountains surrounded by lush gardens, massive banquet halls bustling with beings, and sweeping terraces lined with gilded statues gazing out over endless expanses of land.

"Are they all dead?" Ami whispered.

"Are you confused about where you are, toots?" a woman mocked as we passed by a ballroom filled with dancers, her champagne sloshing. She was wearing a dress that was the sort of brightly colored, flapper-style ensemble one might expect to see on a dancer at a speakeasy. "This is the underworld. We're all dead here!"

"You're lost, sweetheart," the man with her cackled.

They moved their feet in delight as they stomped and whirled in time to the music.

"Speak for yourself," Archie told her snidely.

When I looked up at her, I realized she was

correct—we were surrounded by the dead in this underworld palace.

"This way," Hades said, interrupting my thoughts.

He led us through double doors into a large room that appeared to be a library or study. It was crammed with shelves upon shelves of ancient-looking books, and every surface was caked in dust.

Hades gave Ayla an amused look when she sneezed.

"Sorry," she said, embarrassed.

The dust vanished from the room as the god of the underworld waved his hand, leaving everything sparkling clean. He then motioned for us to take a seat in a cluster of chairs near the center of the room.

Once seated, I looked around.

The space beyond was massive. It was lavishly decorated with glittering chandeliers, lavish tapestries, and gilded furniture, as was the rest of the palace. But it was the massive throne at the far end of the room that drew my attention, carved from a single piece of obsidian and inlaid with rubies that glowed like embers. At its feet was a matching ottoman..

I couldn't help but wonder what secrets might

hide in this library. What did Hades store within these ancient books and scrolls? And why was he bringing us here?

"This is my home, my sanctuary, and my power source all rolled into one," he said deliberately, as if he had heard my question. "It is here that I rule over the dead and use my immense magic." He gave Ayla a friendly smile. "I also keep all of my secrets hidden from prying eyes here."

Why did he look at Ayla when he said that?

Althea looked at Ami, and her eyes grew wide. "Why did he look at Ayla when he said that?" Althea whispered to Ami, echoing the question in my mind.

Ami shook her head. "I don't know."

Ayla's expression shifted from friendly to uncertain. Her eyes darted between Hades and me, her wide eyes finally settling on me for a second. "I want to go home," she whispered.

Althea and Ami shot Ayla looks of surprise.

"Me too," I told her.

"I just feel weird." She pressed her hands to her hips and seemed to take an extra breath, as if she were trying to appear composed.

"Don't worry," Hades said softly. "You are safe —I promise."

"Just don't eat the popcorn," Ami mumbled.

I hushed her. Hades had said nothing about Lothian and Ami being subject to him, and if he didn't know I didn't think we needed to tell him. "Why did you bring us here?" I asked him.

Hades smiled at me, his eyes glowing with an intense energy. "As I said, this room protects my secrets," he said. "It will protect you until we can determine what is going on as well." He walked toward the door. "I will need to lock this door behind me when I go. I hope you understand."

"Wait."

Hades looked at me.

"If these are all your secrets, why do you trust us in here with them?" I tilted my head. "I would think this is the last place you'd want to leave a bunch of strangers."

Hades looked at me for a long moment before answering. "I have my reasons," he said finally. And with that—and with no more explanation— he left the room, locking the door behind him.

As soon as Hades left the room, Archie flapped his wings on my shoulder and cleared his throat. "Well, that was awkward," he said, swiveling his head. "I just want to point out this whole thing is looking less and less like my fault."

CHAPTER TWELVE

"*C*ome on, Lily, spill it," I said to the snowy white owl. "Your goddess lives in the underworld. You have to know more about what's going on than you're saying."

She tucked her head under her wing.

"Lily!"

"Hey, don't yell at my owl!" Althea snapped at me.

She pulled her head out and glanced at the floor. "I know as much as you do," she huffed. "Hecate only tells me what she wants me to know."

"And what does she want you to know?" I asked.

Lily sighed and shook her head. "I don't know.

She just told me I was going to be bonded to her new priestess and to keep an eye on you and make sure you don't get yourself killed."

"You as in me?" I frowned.

"You, as in all of you." The owl clicked her beak in annoyance. "I know it's not much, but it's all I can tell you."

I flopped down like an unstrung puppet on the jeweled ottoman and exhaled. Lily was as concerned as a football coach after a game, and her nonchalance annoyed me.

Ayla, who was sitting in the chair near the window, watched me with amusement. "You're never going to get anything out of her," she said. "She's Althea's. Have Althea ask her."

"I will not harass her." Althea said, and then she turned and glared at me. "She said all she knows."

I took a deep breath and leaned, sinking back into the throne that was the centerpiece of Hades' library. Surrounded by rows of shelves and cabinets that seemed to stretch out forever, I was still amazed we had made it this far without permanent damage to any of us—let alone that I was now looking at the secrets of the Lord of the Dead.

I sat up.

That still didn't seem right.

Why was I looking at the secrets of the Lord of the Dead?

"Hey, what's the relationship between Hades and Hecate?" Ami asked. "I don't remember, exactly. Are they friends, dating, what?"

"Isn't Hades in love with someone? He has a wife or something, right?" Ayla asked. "It's not Hecate, though."

Ami chuckled. "Right. Like any of these gods heard of monogamy."

"Hera's heard of monogamy," I pointed out.

"Oh, right." Ayla tilted her head. "I forgot. She's the god of women, marriage, and childbirth, right?"

"And revenge on cheating husbands," I told her.

Ayla eyed me suspiciously. "For real?"

"You read the stories. Tell me she isn't."

Ami nodded affirmatively. "Astra's not wrong."

"Anyway, Hades and Hecate? They're cousins, I think. Hades is the son of Titans; she's a Titan that got to stay a god when Zeus showed up," Althea said as she scratched her owl behind the ears. "Hecate's powers extended beyond the boundaries of the sky, earth, seas, and underworld."

"Hence, witchcraft," Archie said.

"When Hades kidnapped Demeter's daughter, Hecate played a minor role," I said. "She's also…" I trailed off, sitting up. "Huh. Hecate? She's got a… friend in the underworld, but I can't quite place the name her buddy. Huh. They're companions. I'm sure of it."

"Why did you say it like that?" Ayla asked.

I wasn't sure.

Ami jumped in when I didn't answer. "Hecate is the goddess of magic, witchcraft, the night, light, ghosts, necromancy, and the moon," Ami said. "That much I remember. That, and Hecate's most sacred animal was the dog." She looked down at the wolves sleeping in a puppy pile with the hell hound. "Hey, speaking of—did anyone else notice that key chain Hecate had?"

Ayla tilted her head. "The one with the trident?"

"Yeah," Ami said. "That's Poseidon's symbol. Not Hecate's." Everyone in the room was quiet as they took in the information. Ami leaned back on her heels and nodded, muttering once more, "Yeah."

"Okay, we all spotted it. But what does that mean?" Ayla asked finally.

Ami shrugged. "I don't know, but it can't be good."

Archie nodded. "Hecate is often depicted with three heads or three faces, and her most common symbols are the crossroads and the dog."

"Just thought you'd throw that out there?" I asked.

"I know things," he snapped at me.

Ayla sat up straighter in her chair. "So, the crossroads could represent decisions," she drawled.

"And it could mean my owl was just showing off."

She turned and looked at the books on the wall. "You know, we have all this information. Maybe we should start researching some of this stuff instead of sitting here racking our brain for facts that may or may not be relevant."

"Oh, I don't think we should touch Hades' books," Ami said. "I already ate underworld popcorn and got stuck here. I don't want to get thrown into a torture pit on top of that."

"Why would he leave us in here if he didn't want us to read the books?" Ayla asked.

She had a point.

"Okay," I said. "But we should be careful. No touching anything that looks like it might be trapped."

"And that would look like?" Ayla stared at me expectantly.

Well. How was I supposed to know?

She waited, but no one spoke up. "Right. That's what I thought."

* * *

AYLA STOOD up and approached the bookshelves, her eyes scanning the titles. "If we want to get home, we need to find out what he wants. Maybe these books have the answer," Ayla said. She pulled out one book after another, flipping through the pages as if she was searching for a particular text.

I rose from my chair and wandered through the library. The shelves were filled with tomes of all shapes and sizes. I ran my fingertips over the smooth leather of one book, wondering what secrets lay hidden within those pages.

"Well, I wasn't zapped," I said. I pulled down a book at random. "The Mysteries of Hecate: History, Lore, and Magic" seemed a good place to start. I flipped through the pages of the ancient text, but all the pages were blank.

"You, too?" Althea asked, glancing over at my book. She held hers up. "I got nothing here, either."

"Well, that's weird." Ami grabbed a book from the shelf, flipped it open, and stared. "I don't get it. Why have them all here if they're just blank?"

Ayla looked at Ami oddly. "It's not blank."

"Of course it is." Ami showed Ayla. "Look."

"I'm looking." Ayla pointed at the blank page in Ami's book. "I think this is a drawing of Hecate." she said. "That's actually pretty cool. It's so detailed—you can see her three heads, and even her magical staff."

We all crowded around to look at the supposedly intricate drawing, but there was no intricate drawing. "I see nothing, Ayla," Althea said.

"What do you mean? It's right there!" she insisted. "Go closer to the throne. Maybe you need more light."

"It's not the light, Ayla," I said.

Ami nodded. "We can't see anything." She looked at Althea. "You're priestessed to Hecate, and it's supposedly a drawing of her. Can you see anything at all?"

Althea shook her head.

"What about you two?" I asked the owls.

They shook their feathered heads no.

Ayla's mouth dropped open and her eyes widened. "No way," she said. She kept looking back and forth between us. "You guys are messing with me, right?"

We all shook our heads, and she stepped back.

"I don't get it," she mumbled.

I didn't get it, either, but I was thinking there was definitely something to it.

Ayla continued to flip through the book, pointing out other drawings of Hecate we couldn't see. She pulled other books down and described their contents. She looked at us hopefully each time, holding the open book out, but each time we had to tell her we could see nothing.

Ayla sat down on the floor with a book in her lap and stared at the pages. "It's so annoying," she said. "I can see all of this information, but I'm not sure what it all means. And I'm not sure how you can get it so you can—" Ayla's shot up in mid-sentence as the book slid out of her lap and crashed to the floor. "I've got it! Astra! Read me!"

She thrust her arm at me.

I frowned.

I'd avoided psychically reading my sisters for a reason.

Ayla, especially, was filled with a deep well of thoughts and feelings—history, magic, teenage angst, and more—all swirling around inside her head like a twister. I couldn't control what I saw. Ayla likely couldn't, either.

But what other choice did we have, really?

"Are you sure?" I asked.

She nodded.

I took her hand and took a deep breath.

* * *

As soon as I touched her, I felt a jolt of energy course through me. Ayla's thoughts and knowledge came rushing into my mind, and I gasped at the force of it all.

"Take a deep breath, kid," I told her. "Relax."

As her excitement ratcheted down to a manageable level, the images took shape. I could see the drawings, could sense the words hidden in those pages even if they flipped by so quickly I couldn't quite read them. It was like connecting with another world, a magical realm of secrets and mysteries.

"I see them," I said.

As soon as I informed my sisters of the first mild success, though, the images disappeared and a new scene appeared in my mind. Swirling fog obscured—

Wait a minute.

Mom?

It was Mom, only younger, standing in a circle of light in…in the center of this very room, her staff in one hand and a torch in the other. I felt a powerful presence behind me and turned to see the underworld god himself.

Hold up.

Mom and Hades know each other?

"Minerva, my sweet, how long it has been since you last graced my presence?" Hades asked. He touched her cheek, but she stepped back.

"Don't you 'my sweet' me, you cheating cad. None of that," Mom told him. "I only came here to talk to you."

"Did you?" he asked in a smolderingly sexy voice.

Oh, ew.

I loosened my grip on Ayla's arm slightly, but Archie hissed, "Astra, concentrate."

I clenched my teeth and tried to focus on the scene unfolding in my mind's eye. My head pounded as I witnessed my mother's confrontation with her lover and prayed that Althea could cook up a potion that would wipe it all from my mind when this was done.

"You promised me our daughter wouldn't have any powers that marked her as different in the witch world, but she's got two major powers, Hades—teleporting and death speaking." Mom frowned and pointed her staff at him. "You promised!"

A tingle spread through my body as I processed my mother's words.

Daughter?

"And I have kept my promise," Hades said. "She can not travel to the underworld like you do. And as for her death speaking..." He shrugged. "It is a power that any of my children would have. Obviously. It is not unique to her."

I felt Ayla's arm tense.

"What am I supposed to do with a baby who can talk to the dead and teleport at will? She's going to stand out, Hades. She's going to be different."

"You could say that of all your daughters," he responded, clearly not concerned.

"Ma no happy? Man make Mama mad?"

I gasped.

Sitting at my mother's feet, baby Ayla glanced

up at my mother in confusion, her baby forehead scrunched with worry. My gazed down at the the Ayla of the past and smiled sadly. "No, sweetheart, Mama's not happy, but it'll all be fine. Don't you worry."

"Minerva." Hades shook his head slowly. "I never promised you that your daughter would be just like any other witch. How could you expect that?"

"Our daughter," Mom snapped back.

"I am not the one that seems to forget that." Hades leaned forward and stared at my mother until her eyes dropped. In a voice that echoed with eons of control, he said, "I know that. No one can know. And you know that. Once a year, bring her to—"

"No, Hades," my mother cut him off. "We're done. You know how I feel about having any kind of relationship with you. I don't like it, I don't want it, and I'm not willing to risk my own daughter's safety for it. Especially not—"

"You forget yourself," Hades said, his face growing slightly angry. "I am not asking for much. I just wish to know her and—"

"No."

The images abruptly disappeared right after I felt a sharp pain in my hand. I opened my eyes to see dark red blood trickling out of my palm where Ayla's fingernail had just dug in. My sister, who had been leaning over my hand, slowly rose to look me in the face. "I'm so sorry." She was blushing hot and there was a gleam of worry in her eyes.

I smiled at her. "It's okay. I've had worse."

Ayla took a deep breath and let it out slowly. "Sorry," she repeated. "I just…I'm…I mean…"

"It's okay," I told her more emphatically. "It was an accident."

"Yeah." She shook her head slowly from side to side as if barely able to speak, and then looked at the throne. "Sounds like I was, too, maybe."

"What does that mean? Someone want to tell us what happened?" Ami asked. Her expression was a mixture of fright, disbelief, and confusion. She looked at me. "What did you see?"

I looked at Ayla. It wasn't my secret to tell.

Ayla ran a hand through her black hair and glanced at Ami. "Hades?"

"Yeah."

"He's my father."

CHAPTER THIRTEEN

I knew that as Ayla matured, she became increasingly uncomfortable in our family and with the goddess Athena's service; she could see the dead and teleport objects at will, two extraordinary skills that, when combined in one person, made her stand out. And, I guess, worried Mom, since she was hardly allowed to use either of them.

Despite Mom's efforts to keep Ayla from overusing her powers (particularly the death speaker ones), my sister was determined to prove herself. She worked tirelessly to hone her skills and talents, pushing herself to the snapping point at times in order to grow stronger. She only became somewhat comfortable when—

"Astra, did she?" Ami asked, busting through my thoughts.

"I'm sorry, what?

"Did Mom say why she kept Ayla's parentage from her?" Ami pressed, a look of concern on her face. "Did you overhear anything that would help Ayla understand why—"

"Are you kidding me?" Althea answered for me, glaring at Ami. "Do you know who your father is? Do any of us? Somewhere along the line, Mom decided Ayla was better off not knowing. Oh, no, wait." Althea whirled on me. "You're almost twenty years older than Ayla. She decided none of us should know a damn thing about where we—"

"Althea, this isn't the time for a nervous—"

Althea whirled on Ami. "Don't you dare." I could almost feel her temperature rise as she considered how much this revelation implied that our mother had kept secret from us. "How could she keep something like this from Ayla?" Althea seethed, her hands curled into fists at her sides. "Who's illegitimate kid am I, then?"

Lily leaned her delicate head toward Althea. "I would guess Zeus, but that isn't really an informed answer. It's solely based on his prodigious fathering of demigods."

"Well, I would guess Circe because she's the goddess of potions, but since she's a goddess, I don't see how that would happen," Archie volunteered as he leaned forward. "Come to think of it," he said, his voice hushed, as if he was revealing a secret that was forbidden to speak aloud, "it's crazy that Hecate was the one that came and plucked you from Athena. I mean, sure, you're a witch, but you're not really a Hecate-type witch, know what I mean?" He blinked slowly. "Althea?"

We all stared at him.

His gaze fell to the floor. "Then again, sometimes these things just happen, no?" Archie added quietly. "Someone—something—wants you and you end up with…well, whatever."

He shrugged and went back to staring.

"Can we focus on what's important right now?" I asked, raising my voice to get the group's attention. "Like the fact that we were teleported into the underworld by a toy, and it turns out Hades is Ayla's father? That seems like—"

"A ha!" Archie shouted.

"A ha?"

"I knew this wasn't my fault!" Archie hooted.

We stared at him again.

"Sorry."

"As I was saying, the rest of us are probably not the daughters of gods," I told Althea. "None of us have two major witchcraft powers like Ayla does. Mine's psychometry, Ami sees things, you mix things. The two major powers could be a demigod thing."

Althea stared at Ayla. "Jeez. You're a freaking demigod."

"No, she's our sister," Ami said, her gaze flitting from person to person for a moment. She looked at Ayla. "Astra has had a god in her gut for over a year now. It changes nothing."

"Yeah, especially when Astra barely uses her powers," Althea mumbled.

I glared at her. "I've saved your life, you know."

"Yeah, yeah, I know," Althea grumbled. "I'm sorry. I just…I'm not sure how I feel about this. It's kind of intense."

"It's intense for you? It's not even happening to you!" Ayla replied with a derisive snort. "Think about how I feel. I don't know what to think. I don't know what to feel."

I winced. "Ayla—"

"Don't, okay?" my sister said, actually indignant. "Don't act like what I'm going through is the same thing as what you went through with the star power and all that. You got chosen. I got lied to and abandoned."

"Don't you think that's a little dramatic?" Ami rolled her eyes. "Oh, for goodness' sake, you did not get abandoned. You have a home and a family."

"It's also not really the point," Lily added. "Ayla's powers are stronger than the rest of yours. That's the point, I would think. Well, the only one that matters."

The wolves sat on their haunches, staring at us with interest. As my sisters and I alternated between light squabbling and attempted emotional support, I finally realized how easy it was to forget that these strange and powerful creatures could understand us.

I leaned down and thrust my hand into Lothian's fur.

"Well?" I thought.

"I don't think this is about your owl," Lothian responded. "Well, not completely. Ayla is Hades' daughter, Althea's oathed to another underworld goddess." Lothian's gaze flicked to Ami. "If I had to place a bet, someone is going to show up for your seer sister over there any minute now."

Lothian's words echoed in my mind as I

stared at my sisters. "What do you mean, this isn't completely about my owl?" I asked him.

"Your mother couldn't speak to you easily back at the house," he said as he looked around the room, and then stared at the door. "Something prevented her. Then your goddess Athena made Ami's card glow for Archie. As much as I'm not a fan, she is generally the wisest and most levelheaded of the gods."

"So the myths say." I wouldn't know.

Never met the woman.

"If that's the case, why would she need to send you a star card for Archie to aid him in a test she ordered and designed? That continues to nag at me, Astra. It makes no sense at all." He nosed my hand. "Think about it."

"I'M SO glad I found you!"

Ace shot through the door to the library like he was being pursued by a pack of werewolves. On his tail was a woman I hadn't seen before—and I would have remembered her. She was bright and glowing, and her eyes sparkled with a life I had never seen in anyone's eyes before. "I was beginning to fear that I would find nothing but the scent of you. And maybe not even that."

"Oh, really?" Althea looked at him suspiciously. "You left us in the middle of nowhere, buddy. Why would you care one way or another what happened to us?"

Lothian growled, and I had to agree.

Raising an eyebrow, he brushed a wild lock of hair behind his ear and winked at my sister. "Of course I care! I've been looking for you all for over two hours," he said. "You can't believe the trouble I had getting down here from the barrier. I got stuck in this water tunnel that just kept flowing in one direction, and—" He looked at the woman with him and shrugged. "Well, anyway, I thought I was going to be down there for hours. I almost gave up." His gaze flicked to the wolves, then the hell hound, and then to Archie. "I'm glad I didn't."

I noticed he didn't look at Lily.

"Who is this?" Ayla asked, pointing.

The woman behind him was difficult to ignore. She had a ponytail of brightly colored strands of yellow and red threaded through her chin-length, wavy blond hair. Her big, green eyes seemed to radiate light, and her tan suggested she had been out in the sun for some time despite the perpetual darkness of this place.

"Yeah, who are you?" Althea asked.

She squinted back and then stepped forward. There was a pregnant pause as we all weathered glances of uncertainty, the woman smiling confidently as she took her place among us. The room had suddenly become eerily quiet.

We waited.

The woman smiled knowingly at us, twirling a red flower between her fingers.

Was she here with Ace for a reason? Or was this the newest paranormal to join this strange journey, the one that would affect Ami's life by action or information?

"What's your name?" I asked the woman.

"I have many names."

"You do?" Lily asked, her voice dripping with disbelief. "Are you sure?"

Okay, that animosity was unexpected.

"I do," the woman told Lily. The woman did not volunteer what those many names might be. She turned away from the owl and looked at Ami. "Have you met with Hades yet? Ace told me you intended to search for him hoping he would assist you in leaving this place."

Huh.

I surveyed the room, as if it would address my confusion. Hades claimed this place was his secret hideaway, protected by his minions and defended by the very lack of knowledge of its existence. Or so I thought.

He definitely said it was a secret.

If this place is what he claimed, what are these people doing moseying in like its nothing?

"We did, but we didn't get around to talking about the whole leaving thing quite yet," Ami said, her gaze more curious than hostile. "I feel like I know you from somewhere. Do I know you from somewhere?"

"Not really." She smiled. The expression was friendly, but behind it lay some dark kernel of emotion I couldn't identify. "I'm here to give you a choice and to tell you something. The test is whether you wish me to do so."

Ami looked startled. "Me?"

I swallowed hard as I met Lothian's glance.

"A choice of what?" Ami asked.

I felt like I was standing on the banks of a river, watching as Ami rowed closer and closer to the next bend. I knew the water here was deep and getting deeper. I wanted to warn her, but it was like I could do nothing except silently implore her to stop.

"A choice of who," the woman corrected. She glanced at Ace. "To get what you want, another must come. You may or may not want to say who that will be. You may not even want to wait. Perhaps you want to return home before even knowing?"

"I don't understand."

The cryptic words were making my anxiety rise, and I struggled to speak. "Wait," I said. "Wait for who?"

Blondie ignored me.

"I don't understand," Ami said, with an edge of panic. "What are you asking me?"

"You don't have to understand. That's not required in this place," the woman told her. "You can choose not to say anything. But it would be better if you did." The woman smiled. "Do you want to wait and see what occurs, or do you choose a path home?"

"Oh! Wait—so we can leave the underworld?" Ami asked, her voice rising with excitement. "Even me? Lothian, too? You're here to tell me we can leave the underworld?"

The woman smiled. "I'm here to give you a choice."

"Are you not concerned about this?" Archie hissed at me.

"I am, but what am I supposed to do?" I hissed back. "It's Ami's test, and Ami's choice. She's likely to understand it better than anyone else. It's not my test."

"Now, suddenly, you're a mythology expert." Archie gave me a dirty look and clacked his beak at me. "You're right. You're probably right. Or it's a trick, and she's about to condemn us to Tartarus for eternity. You know, one of the two."

"You and the werewolf have eaten food in the underworld," the mysterious woman said. "You know what that means, right?"

"Yes," Ami replied.

"You can't leave without paying the price," Blondie said. "Neither of you can. So, your first choice is to stay. You and the wolf stay here in the underworld, as is proper for one who has eaten of it's food."

"Am I choosing for both of us?" Ami asked, glancing at Lothian.

"You are. And if you stay, you will have to remain here," the woman told her. "You will have to stay in the realm of the dead. You will have to exist here, and you will have to move among the dead. Are you willing to do that?"

"Well. No. I'd prefer not to if there's any other option."

"Then the second choice. The number of souls must remain balanced. If you and the wolf will leave, someone must take your places."

"That sounds like a good deal," Althea said, her gaze flickering to me.

"It always sounds like a good deal. It never is. Who decides which two beings replace Ami and Lothian?" I stared at the mystery woman, waiting for her to elaborate.

Her cool gaze met mine. "I said there would be a choice."

* * *

I STARED AT THE WOMAN, my stomach churning. Her words tugged at me, but the cadence of her voice made me nervous, and I wrung my hands. Two thoughts reverberated in my mind: something was wrong, and I was missing something big here.

I hoped the two thoughts weren't about the same thing.

"How does she choose?" I asked, feeling a sense of dread settle in my stomach. Was there something sinister behind her offer? Or was she truly offering Ami and Lothian a chance for freedom from the underworld?

The woman merely smiled again and said nothing more. As her words sank in, I could see that Ami was already sold on getting out of here.

"Uh," Ami said, "how do I choose? Who do I choose?"

"She's not going to tell you," Althea said.

"She will not tell you until the right moment," the woman corrected.

"So we can leave if we say yes?" Ami asked.

"Wait a minute, yes to what?" I asked. "What is Ami agreeing to?"

"You can if you're willing to take the risk," the woman replied directly to Ami. "The risk that you will be replaced. The risk that you will choose someone to take your place. The risk that the person you choose cannot return to the land of the living."

"I don't like that," Ami whispered, her face pale. "It feels wrong."

"Neither do I," I replied.

"Oh, please," Althea said. "This whole thing feels wrong."

"It's not like you deserve to be here any more than some random person who flits through your mind, is it?" Ace said. "Death is inevitable."

Ami looked warily convinced this was the

road to freedom. "And if I don't choose? Then what?" Ami asked.

The woman smiled. "If you don't choose, then you and the wolf will remain here."

"And if I choose, then what?"

"Then you and the wolf will leave, and someone else will take your place."

"And what will they get?" Ami asked. "What's the catch?"

"The catch?" Ace laughed. "They will be dead."

"Is that it?" Ami said. "That's the catch? Just dead. Not punished, not tortured, not shoved headfirst into some boiling lava pit for eternity or placed a foot away from food they can never touch? Just dead?"

"Just dead. That's the catch," the woman replied. "You can stay here, or you can leave. You can be replaced, or you can move on. The choice is yours."

Ami glanced at Lothian. "What do you think?"

The werewolf stepped forward, his eyes flashing. "I think that the entire world would be better off if you left here and went home." He looked up slyly at me. "I'm not sure Astra would agree the same goes for me." His gaze returned to her. "But I have to admit the price is giving me pause. You would kill two people. I'm comfortable with that price, but I am a wolf. I'm not sure it's one you will be able to live with."

I repeated what Lothian said.

"But we don't know that," Ami whispered, her expression twisting in frustration as she tried to find any way her exit ticket wasn't an evil act. "The person I choose might have died, anyway. Heart attack or car accident." She pulled her cards from her pocket and showed them to the wolf. "I mean, I am a seer. I have to be able to find two people whose death is imminent." Ami's gaze flitted from Lothian to me. "What do you think?"

I looked up into the cloudy eyes of the woman standing before me—the unnaturally bright eyes of a divine-touched being. "I think it's a trick."

"I think it's a trick, too," Althea said. And then she shrugged. "But I don't know why. It's like something's nagging at me, just out of reach."

"Oh, right," Ayla said with rolled eyes. "You with the brand new white owl on your arm that you know absolutely nothing about serving the goddess that conveniently showed up in the middle of our underworld kidnapping to talk to you? You think it's a trick?" She snorted. "Well, hold the phone, then."

"It isn't your choice, grumpy, so what do you

care? And hey, at least I didn't murder two people to get the owl," Althea spat back.

"Okay, everyone, just calm down." Althea shot me a dirty look. "Is there anything else we can do to change the situation?" I asked the woman.

The woman just smiled.

"You're out of your depth, Astra," Althea said. "And you know what? I don't care if she's a goddess, a trickster, or the great Oz. I want out. I'm sure Ami does, too. And I'd just like to say one more thing: abduction should not be a right just because someone is divine."

"Amen, sister," Ayla said.

"I agree with Althea," she said, turning toward the woman. "All of this back and forth is making my head hurt." Ami rubbed her head, and murmured, "So help me, goddess, I just want to go home."

The woman leaned forward, a victorious grin on her face. Power surged in the air as her gemstone eyes glowed a haunting turquoise.

Ami's eyes flew open. "What's happening? What did I do?" she cried.

In a flash of green-yellow magic, my mother and Jason Bishop appeared behind the woman with the same look of shock on their faces we, no doubt, had on ours.

"Persephone, what have you done?" my mother whispered.

The goddess laughed.

"Minerva, try to keep your daughters from eating any more popcorn," she said, and then blew Mom a kiss. "We'll see each other soon." A loud pop sounded, followed by a long hiss, and then she and Ace were gone in a plume of sulfur-smelling vapor.

"Persephone?" Ami asked, confused. "Who's Persephone?"

CHAPTER FOURTEEN

*A*mi, Althea, and Ayla shouted "Mom!" at the same time.

I stared at her silently as Lothian bumped against me.

My mother's gaze flicked to each of us, her eyes widening in shock. "What are you all doing here?" she whispered. Her eyes widened as realization passed through her, followed closely by shock and awe. Then she looked down at her body, stunned. "What am I doing here?"

I observed the scene in silence.

"Who's Persephone?" Ami asked.

"Who's—" Mom's eyes widened even further at Ami's question. It was as if the additional shock would pop her eyeballs right out of her head. "Oh, no. No, no, no. It can't be."

"What is it, Ms. Arden?" Jason stroked his chin and furrowed his brow as he looked across from me. "Astra? Where is this? Where are we?"

Before I could answer, Lothian leaped on me, nearly knocking me down. He whined and pawed at my arm. "Whoa," I yelped in surprise. "What the hell?" My free hand fell over the top of his head, gripping into his coarse fur with a rough yank. "What? Can't you see I'm busy?"

"You know, I've disemboweled people for less," he said, fixating me with an icy stare. "None of you seem to know who Persephone is. Althea asked who she was when we were watching the welcome movie, and I thought she was making a joke," Lothian thought, his tongue lolling. "So, let me ask you—do you know who Persephone is?"

"Some chick that died?" I said, shrugging. "I don't know. They didn't explain much in that welcome movie."

A low growl rumbled in his chest. "She's the goddess of spring," Lothian explained. "She married Hades, and she ate a pomegranate seed and couldn't get out of the underworld."

I nodded. "Okay. There' are a lot of minor

deities we didn't learn much about. What's your point?"

"My point is she's the queen of the underworld," Lothian said, his thought accompanied by a low growl. "Persephone is no minor deity. Last year you met Zagreus in Palm Beach? Dionysus?"

I nodded.

"Well, Persephone is his mother," Lothian replied. "This goddess is no minor deity, no footnote story in the myths. Astra, you should know something about her. That you don't? That all of your sisters don't? It's not natural."

"Persephone is the queen of the underworld," I whispered to myself, my gaze moving from Lothian to my mother. "And the wolf thinks she's a goddess I should know. Then why don't I know anything about her?" I rose to my feet and stared at Minerva Arden. "I can barely focus my mind on her name, Mother." I gestured toward my sisters. "I wonder if they can."

Mom's face remained solemn. "Astra—"

"Mom, can I ask you something?" I said, anger in my voice. She looked down. I knew she would. "Why? As far as I can tell, there's only one person on the planet with enough power and connection to us to cast a spell that would block a goddess from our minds," I said, my eyes narrowing. "Only one person has enough trust, love, and magical prowess to remove the thought of this goddess from our minds. All of our minds. Even mine."

She stared back at me.

"Yeah, I don't know who the heck you're talking about, either," Archie said, preening distractedly. "Never heard of Persephone." He tilted his head. "Unless it's that orange fruit that tastes like cinnamon mango?"

"A persimmon?" Jason asked.

"You would immediately think about food, Archie—" As soon as the words left my mouth, I gasped and whirled on my mother. "You poisoned us."

"Oh, Astra, don't be so melodramatic," my mother scoffed at me in annoyance. "I did not poison you. I just made sure that you were protected from Persephone before you went off on the Orphic investigation last year. You and your sisters." Mom looked at Archie. "Once Alexarchos arrived, I needed to make sure we were protected from any vengeful shenanigans by Persephone. Should they occur."

"Why?" Ami asked.

Because Mom diddled around with her husband, that's why, I thought snidely.

"Persephone is a threat to our family, Ami. That woman is only interested in one thing: revenge. So, I cast a quick protection spell and sprinkled it on the deviled eggs with the paprika." My mother looked at the floor in embarrassment. "I didn't expect it would last quite this long."

"Why would this goddess want revenge on Astra? And what did any of this have to do with the three of us? And it never occurred to you to remove it?" Althea said in disbelief. "Hell's bells, Mom! And you tell us we're being irresponsible witches."

"Yes, well, it worked a little too well," Mom said with a heavy sigh. "I am not sure why she should have vanished from your minds for such a long time but...well, nothing can be done about it now."

"I still don't understand. Why?" Ami asked. "Why would you do that?"

I stayed quiet, hoping Mom would confess what Lothian had told me. That Persephone was married to Ayla's father. That had to be the reason.

"I had to," Mom said. "And if you think about

it, it worked out for the best. You were all fully protected for a full year."

Ayla crossed her arms. "Are you daft, woman? We're in hell," she countered. "If you can explain to me how that translates to us being protected, I'm all ears."

"How would that protect them?" Jason asked, his face a mask of befuddlement as he tried to follow what was happening. "They couldn't see danger coming if it was headed straight for them.."

"Obviously, we didn't see danger coming. We're here. You're here," I said. "Maybe I wouldn't have grabbed that stupid pedestal if I'd known—"

"Or maybe if I knew my father was Hades, I could have sensed something in that stupid toy. Some sense of deception, some whiff of the underworld," Ayla said, her voice low and angry.

"I saved you," Mom whispered, her voice low and somber. "I just knew that there was a connection between Persephone and the Orphic investigation, and I hoped I could protect you all from her influence. At least until you had solved the investigation. We needed to help the Orphics, yes, but you didn't need to know—"

"Mom, cut the crap," I said, a wave of nausea

rolling over me. My stomach turned thinking about what she'd done.

"Don't you judge me, Astra Arden! You hardly studied what I taught, anyway. Maybe if you had stayed home where you belonged, I never would have had to take extra steps to protect you all." Mom's words soaked into me like salty water, filling my mouth with a nasty taste.

"Don't you dare blame this on me," I told her.

"Mom, you and Jason are both dead," Althea added. "You realize that, right? Both of you. You're dead. All the excuses in the world, all the finger pointing? It will not change that."

Dead.

Jason is dead.

Mom is dead.

Dead.

The word echoed repeatedly in my mind.

Dead. Dead. Dead. Dead.

My mother and Jason were dead.

* * *

"IT WASN'T PAINFUL, if that's what you're asking," Jason said. The flickering light of the fire danced across his face, glimmering in the strands of hair resting on his forehead, and reflecting in his eyes.

"Honestly, if we all die only once? That was a pretty good way to go. Poof. Just suddenly not there."

He grinned at me, and I smiled back at him.

Leave it to Jason Bishop to make death sound like an unexpected visit to Disney World.

Mom, Althea, Ami, and Ayla sat cross-legged around an open hearth, scowling at each other. Jason and I had taken a seat on a nearby stone bench, and we looked up at the vaulted ceiling covered in an infinite number of stalactites. It formed a strange and menacing canopy above our heads.

"Astra, really," he said, squeezing my hand. "It's okay." As he squeezed, Beethoven's "Moonlight Sonata" played from somewhere outside the room.

"There has to be a way to undo this," I told him.

I looked down at my hand, which was intertwined with Jason's. My imagination had us running along the path near his school, then off-roading in my Jeep. I smiled as I remembered. I looked up at Jason while enjoying the feel of his warm, comforting hand in mine.

"And yet there isn't," he said emphatically, making me shudder. "I'm no longer alive. I'm not sure how I recognize this is permanent, but I do. I died, and it is irreversible." Jason jerked his head toward Mom. "Your mother and I cannot go back."

We undid it for Lothian and Ami...

...but, I reminded myself, their bodies were here.

Mom and Jason...

I shuddered again.

Lothian, snide human jerk but sorta decent werewolf, stood in one corner of the room looking at us. His canine brow was creased in what looked like a tiny frown, as if he couldn't decide what to think about the scene that unfolded before him.

Maybe he was trying to figure out what Jason and I were now.

I know I was.

"Why aren't you freaking out?" I asked.

"What? It's just death. I've been around death all my life. Let's turn that question around. Why aren't you bursting into tears, grieving?" he asked, amused. "You're the one that has to go on without me. If I were in your shoes and the situation was reversed, I'd probably be a mess."

"You are in my shoes, just in the underworld," I pointed out. "I don't know. I think I'm not bursting into tears because I'm still too angry at my mother."

"Oh?"

"That and you look less disappointed about this turn of events than I would have expected a dead man to look."

"Rude," he said, and then laughed. "But true, I guess."

"I can't quite work up the proper amount of sadness right now. It still seems unreal." I paused and looked at Jason's hand once more. It looked so real. It felt real. "I can't believe all this is happening."

"It's done," Jason told me confidently. "There's nothing we can do about it. You can't bring me back to the living world. Well, as a living being, anyway."

"You don't know that—"

"I do. I'm glad you're here to say goodbye, Astra, believe me, I am—but I'm still dead. I can't go back. I'm here, with you, for a little longer and that's okay."

I was shocked by his attitude. I expected someone in his situation to break down into tears. Ask the universe why. Hell, get angry. Instead, he was serene and almost happy.

"You're not upset at all?" I asked.

He shook his head. "I'm not. I'm not upset at all. I'm kind of excited. I mean, I'm dead. I'm from a town that talks to the dead. My mother talks to the dead. I know the dead can leave here—so I'm sure we'll still see each other occasionally."

"We won't, though," I said, shaking my head. "I'm not a death speaker."

"That's right, I forgot." I jumped as Jason burst out laughing. "Oh, Astra. What a thing, huh? We really were just two ships passing in the night heading off to different ports with entirely different agendas and goals, weren't we?"

Ouch.

He wasn't wrong, but I didn't want to admit it.

I also didn't want to admit how much his statement hurt.

"What's happening back at Arden House? After we disappeared, what happened?" I asked, trying to change the subject. I didn't want to think about us being ships.

"Well, that toy was nowhere to be found, and the pedestal was gone. Everyone that came to the party booked out, except for the usual suspects. Eddie and Emma, my mom, the captain." His face fell. "Oh, no. Mom."

"You can talk to her, eventually. But I hope she's as lackadaisical about your death as you seem to be." For all Jason's chipper acceptance, he looked a little concerned about his mother's reaction. "All the paranormals left?"

"Yup. I think they figured if someone as powerful as you four could get plucked out of Arden House in the blink of an eye, then it wasn't exactly safe for them to hang about, either." He looked around. "So, this is the Greek underworld, huh?" Jason asked me. "Wild. I didn't think I'd wind up here."

"Where else would you end up?" I asked him.

"Astra, this isn't the only afterlife," Jason said, laughing. "I've read about Tibetan Buddhists and Hindus and Indigenous Australian Aborigine and Native American and Maori and Mexican and Mayan and Egyptian and—"

"Okay, okay, I get it."

"This isn't even the main one. Think about it. How many people throughout time have believed in a Greek afterlife?" Jason shrugged in that innocent, charming way he had. "I doubt it's all that many. I think I just wound up here because of what Ami did. I mean, people's faith is largely an accident of birth, right? And this wasn't really my belief system." Jason glanced at Ami, who was hollering at my mother. "Which is fine. I mean, this is cool, I guess."

"So where would you have wound up if you weren't here?" I asked. It seemed a strange question to be asking my boyfriend. Especially now that he was already dead.

He thought about it for a second. "Honestly, I don't know," he said. "Our town believes people stay around to help people, so maybe I just would have haunted you?" He smiled. "I don't know."

"Really?"

Jason tilted his head back and forth and his eyes widened, like he was looking at stars on the library ceiling only he could see. "It's weird, Astra. I don't really care about the question anymore. It just doesn't matter." He reached over and took my hand. "I'm where I'm meant to be."

"Hermes?" Ami shouted. "Are you telling me my father is Hermes?!"

* * *

I REMEMBERED the quiet but confident man I met last year, the one who told me I could send messages to the divine realms, the underworld, and the world of mortals—right before unveiling my soldier, Godfree Carrillo. It was a performance intended to persuade me he, Hermes, could do so.

Last year, I didn't believe the gods existed.

It was a much more pleasant time in my life.

Anyway, I'd met Ami's father, Hermes, briefly. He came to Apollo's house last year...huh. Weird. Apollo was the first person to greet us this year once we were teleported from Arden House. A weird coincidence.

I looked at Ami. Her blond hair, her gentle features. I'd met Hermes last year in Palm Beach, and she looked like him.

How did I miss it?

And how much more did I miss?

Ami stood there for a moment after shrieking, her mouth open in shock. Finally, her eyes dropped, and she paced, mumbling to herself.

"This can't be all connected, can it?" I whispered to no one in particular. I pulled my hand from Jason's and scrambled to my feet. "Last year, Godfree said that Mom was getting up there in years—"

"Godfree? Who's Godfree?" my mother asked.

"One of Astra's soldiers when she was in the military," Ayla told her, glancing at Ami with a worried expression. "He's dead, and he came to talk to her at the Cassandra veil-drop thing."

"And last year at Yule," Althea added. "She told me."

"Yes, Hermes—Ami's father—brought him," I said as I marched toward her. "I met Hermes, Mom. At Dell's—um, Apollo's—house in Palm Beach." Archie squeezed my arm to keep himself steady, and I looked at him suspiciously. "You're awfully quiet. Did you know any of this?"

"Yeah, so, you know how I tell you I know everything all the time, bragging about what a big brained owl I am?" His stem gaze met my own suspicious one.

"Yes?"

"I lied."

I stared at him.

He stared back. "What?"

"We're going to have a talk about this later. For now, though," I whirled on my mother, "I need to know what else you're hiding?" I asked her as I joined my three sisters in a confrontational line in front of our (apparently somewhat divinely promiscuous) mother. "That covers Ayla and Ami. What about Althea?"

"You don't understand how this works," my mother said with frustration. "None of you girls ever truly understood the amount of politics between the gods. They're fighting each other for dominance. They're fighting each other for terrain and power and—"

"We get it. It's complicated. So why the heck are you sleeping with them?" I asked. "Why didn't you tell us?"

"You're all too young to have been told about it!" she shouted at me.

"I'm in my midthirties!" I shouted back. "I know where babies come from!"

"Why can't you just tell us the complete story?" Ami asked. "The entire story of your life, Mom? Where we all came from?"

"Well, darling, you know I'm not a big fan of sharing," she said. "And it's more than that. I told you. I'm trying to protect you. All of you."

Ayla gestured around the room and rolled her eyes. "Great job."

"Yeah, I mean, hell seems safe," Althea said dryly.

"Stop! You're both still children, and you have no right to talk to me that way. I will not apologize for keeping my children safe." Mom shook her head. "I did what I had to do to keep you girls safe."

We stared at her.

When we didn't respond, she added, "That's that."

"You really amaze me. You think a lifetime of secrets can be solved in fifteen minutes with a stomp of your foot and an assurance of requirement," I said. "You kept all of us under lock and key and completely ignorant of any tie to anyone other than you. That's not 'that.' That's a problem. That deserves an explanation. And answers."

"How could you not tell me Hades was my father?" Ayla asked, circling back to the wound in her that cut the deepest.

"Oh, Ayla, when I left your father," she said, "he tried to kill me."

For a second, I was too shocked to even speak, and I felt horribly guilty. "Are you saying Hades abused you?" I asked gently.

She looked at me as if I had lost my mind. "Of course not," she said sharply as her mouth tightened into a thin, angry line. "Hades wanted me to stay here with him eternally. But I had three young daughters at home, so I had to return." We stared at her. "What was I going to do, leave you with Gwen?"

Althea's mouth dropped. "Wow, Mom. You must have thought about it since you had that option at the ready."

"Althea—"

"She always has options at the ready, don't you, Minerva?" an old woman's voice said. "I told you that your secrets would come to this, Minerva."

My mother's face turned white.

We all fell silent as we watched the crone enter, her face looking both young and old. My mother winced with each tap of her carved cane against the floor like it was the ticking down of a bomb about to explode.

"Grandma?" Ami whispered.

"Oh, snap," Ayla added.

"You are correct, Ami, love." As she walked toward us, the woman's wrinkled hands grabbed the cane. "I told your mother keeping secrets from her daughters would come to no good." She sighed. "And look where we've gotten ourselves."

"I did what I had to do, Mother," my mother said with a weighty finality after she reluctantly pulled her gaze toward my unhappy grandmother.

"Did you? I told you that your secrets would come to this, Minerva," Gran said once more like it was a rote. "Thus we find ourselves."

CHAPTER FIFTEEN

I haven't mentioned my granny much.

My grandmother was a strict but loving woman. She was always well-dressed, with coiffed hair and impeccable makeup. A bit of a snob, maybe? And she didn't suffer fools at all. I loved her dearly—while she was keen to chastise me if I misbehaved, she was also swift to offer a kind word and a hug when I needed it.

She was a strong witch, and I looked up to her.

She died peacefully in her sleep in her Arden House bedroom when I was six years old, with no pain or suffering. Much more incredible, she had vanished right in front of my eyes—there was no body to bury. Gram had magically taken care of everything.

The days following her death were a blur, filled with tears and sadness. Even in my childhood grief, I couldn't help but feel a sense of wonder and amazement at the unexpected way she had left this world. It was the first time I realized we were different from everyone else.

Gran's passing on had a significant impact on my mom. She was devastated by the news, and it appeared to my young mind that in her grief, she became even more controlling and overbearing. She was constantly concerned about me and watched my every move.

Things only got worse as I got older. Over time, my mother became more domineering and obsessive. I might have felt sorry for her had it been a passing phase, a temporary reaction to trauma.

But it wasn't.

She transformed herself into an authoritarian force who ruled our family with an iron fist, and when my sisters were born, she smothered them as well.

"Grandma!" Ayla yelled. My youngest sister dashed across the room and wrapped her arms around the older woman. "How come you haven't come to meet me? Did you know I'm a death speaker?" she asked, astonished. Grandma glanced at Mom, her expression brimming with disapproval. "Aunt Gertie hangs out with us now," she explained. "I mean, really, she lives with us in a way. Don't you ever talk to her? How come you never came by?"

"It's a long story, kiddo. One that doesn't make your mother look all that good, and she's got enough to deal with right now. Trust me, I've watched over all of you girls," Grandma said, patting Ayla on the head. "And I'm here now where you can see me. That's all that matters."

"No." Ayla frowned and stepped back. "No way," she said. "Hold the phone. Are you saying Mom blocked you from Arden House the way she blocked Aunt Gertie?"

My mother and one of her sisters had a disagreement when they were teenagers. In retaliation, my mother blocked her sister from ever communicating with us from the great beyond.

Aunt Gertie could eventually break through and let Ayla know she was there, but for much of our lives, we didn't even know there were three Arden sisters in a generation up.

"I did not say that, but you are very

perceptive, little Ayla. Maybe your mother wants to take this one," Grandma hedged, giving Mom a pointed look. "After all, she hasn't brought a single hidden issue into the light voluntarily. No time like the present to give that a go, eh?"

My mother turned red with anger and embarrassment, but she said nothing. She just glared at my grandmother as Hades slipped into the room, his lanky shadow stretching toward the curved walls. He surveyed the room with a cool, assessing gaze.

My mother scowled and turned toward him, clearly seething with rage. "Hades! This is your fault! You promised me you would never tell them!" Mom shouted at Hades. "All of this is your fault!"

Hades remained calm in the face of my mother's anger. He simply raised an eyebrow and said coolly, "No, it isn't and no, I didn't. This is a culmination of your choices, Minerva. Not mine."

My mother scoffed, clearly not believing him. She glared at the god with a mixture of anger and frustration. "We're here in your realm. How is this not your—"

"There is no need to blame me, dear," he said calmly. "I am not responsible for your choices."

"But you are responsible for this!" my mother

spat, gesturing wildly at the surrounding library. "You knew who those girls were the moment they crossed into the underworld! You should have contacted me!"

Hades raised an eyebrow.

"His diabolically adorable eyebrow is trying to remind you of your penchant for blocking people from Arden House, and from your daughters, Minerva," Grandma said, her voice dripping with censure. "You can't keep running from the truth forever, and you can't keep blaming others for your own mistakes."

"I didn't want this, Minerva."

My mother seethed in silence as Hades watched her with a cool, unreadable expression on his face. I saw a glimmer of sadness and regret in his eyes.

I wondered what sadness and regret a god had.

The atmosphere in the library was heavy and tense as my mother stared at Hades, her gaze full of animosity and resentment. She was clearly not happy about the way things had turned out.

But to my utter shock, Mom slowly and reluctantly hung her head in defeat.

"Fine. I know I have been wrong with some of my calls," she breathed. "I know I have made a few mistakes with my daughters and the gifts they possess. But I meant to protect them."

Gram laughed heartily at this.

Mom's cheeks pinked. "I did! Once I chose a path, I had to commit to that path. It's our way."

"It's your way," my grandmother said flatly.

I'll give Mom one thing.

She was a veritable force of nature, and she was tenacious in her self-righteous defense of herself. She stood defiant as her mother judged her. She faced Hades even as he watched my mother intently, his piercing gaze taking in and weighing every word and gesture she made.

"We've evolved," Hades told Mom. "You and Athena have not evolved. But I understand. You have lived in a world of hidden secrets for so long, it's hard to break free. And it's even harder when you are forced to confront the consequences of your actions. But that is where we are now, Minerva—we're here, together, facing the truth head on. In the end, it is what this place is for, after all."

"Will you listen to his words of wisdom and learn from them? Or will you continue down the same destructive path that has brought us to this point in your afterlife, too?" my grandmother asked her.

My mother hung her head, tears streaming down her face, and my sisters and I watched this all unfold in front of us. In some ways, it had nothing to do with us.

In another way?

It had everything to do with us.

"You're a strong woman," Hades said gently. "But you've been living in the past for too long. You have missed out on so much because of your unwillingness to let go of your old ways."

Jeez, where the hell were these guys twenty years ago when I wished "ancient advice" Minerva would get all the way off my back?

Oh, right.

She'd warded our very lives against them.

Yep.

Typical Mom.

I sighed, throwing her a lifeline. "Look, Mom, we all make mistakes," I said. "It's never too late to learn from them and grow as a person. Our destiny is not set in stone; it can be shaped by our own actions. You are still in control of your own destiny, your own afterlife."

Hades smiled briefly. "You are wise, Astra, daughter of Apollo."

If Sisyphus' boulder dropped from the sky and rolled over me, I would have been less surprised.

* * *

Hades is Zeus's brother. Hermes and Apollo are both children of Zeus. So, Hades was uncle to my father, Apollo, making the god of the underworld…my great-uncle?

Maybe.

Hermes was Apollo's cousin.

No, wait. Half brother.

Oh, jeez, I think they're cousins and half brothers. Sort of.

My head was spinning.

"What about Althea?" I asked. "Who's Althea's father?"

"Hades, please, don't," my mother whispered.

Hades' eyes drifted to her, and I saw a flicker of something in them. Compassion? Sadness? Regret? He turned toward Althea and gently caressed her cheek. "You are the daughter of my brother, Poseidon, god of water, earthquakes, and horses."

"You mean god of the sea," Archie corrected.

"I said what I said, owl," Hades responded.

Archie looked down.

"Somehow, that totally tracks if you think about it," Ayla observed.

Suddenly, Althea froze and then whirled on

me. "Wait a minute, wait a minute, hold up, hold the phone," she said, snapping her fingers. "We met my father today." Her eyes got big as she looked at me. "And your father! That was your father!"

I nodded.

"Why didn't they say anything?"

"I don't know."

"He's my father?" she asked, her voice barely above a whisper.

I nodded again. "Ayla's right. It makes sense."

"Oh, my gods," she said, sinking down onto the stone floor. "No wonder I always felt like I didn't quite fit in anywhere. I always thought it was because I was a witch. Or maybe a changeling baby. Or secretly adopted. But it wasn't that at all. It was because we were all different. We all must have felt like we didn't belong." She looked up at Mom, her eyes filled with tears. "You said our fathers were dead or gone or disappeared or didn't care or left or— Mom, how could you do that?"

Mom looked crestfallen. "Althea—"

"No!" Althea turned away from us, her shoulders shaking. I touched her, but she shrugged me off. Then Mom reached out to touch her arm, but Althea shrugged her off even more violently. "Don't you touch me," she said coldly. "Just don't."

Mom wiped a tear away. "But Althea—"

"I can't believe you would keep these things from us. This wasn't just something you didn't tell us. These were things you actively kept from us. Worked to hide from us. Parts of who we are. You worked against us coming to the truth!"

Mom watched Althea as she walked toward the fire, and then glared at Hades.

"She'll be okay," Ayla whispered.

"Will she?" Ami asked. "Will you? Will I?"

No one answered her.

I couldn't at that moment. I was in shock.

My father was Apollo.

Althea's father? Poseidon.

Ami's father? Hermes.

Ayla's father? Hades, god of the underworld.

I wiped my eyes as tears threatened to fall.

I wondered if Aunt Gwennie knew. How deep did the secrets in our family go? Was Aunt Gwennie voluntarily staying silent, or did my mother bespell her as well? Did Aunt Gertie know what my mother had done? Or did Mom bind the ghost from speaking of it the way she kept the specter of our aunt away from us most of our lives?

And what of these divine men that stayed away, that said nothing until the past few days? Even though I met two a year ago…

I had a lot of questions.

One thing I didn't have a question about, though.

I knew that no matter our fathers, we were still strong women in our own right. And together, we would weather this storm and emerge stronger than ever before.

* * *

OKAY, so maybe I was a little rattled.

When Hades asked to speak in private, I felt rattled.

"Sure," I answered, " but I'm not going to call you Uncle Hades. I hope you understand."

I looked at him—really looked at him—for the first time since this chaos began. We were tucked into a corner behind several book shelves, and he stood against the wall, leaning his back on the stones.

"I understand," he assured me. "I want you to know I am here for you, Astra. All of you. Even if you don't want to call me family."

The god's eyes were piercing, and he exuded a

sense of authority that made me slightly nervous —like he could plunge me into a pit of lava in the blink of an eye. But he also had a kind expression on his face, and I could see compassion in his eyes.

"It just feels weird, you know? You're technically my great-uncle, I think, but you're also the god of the underworld, so that's a little weird." Somewhere in my mind, I realized I was babbling nervously. (I may have been babbling, but my owl was stock still and silent on my shoulder.) "You also look younger than me, so. Yep. It'd just be too confusing."

Hades chuckled softly. "I can imagine this all must be quite confusing for you. But I assure you, I am comfortable with whatever you wish to call me."

Awesome. "Awesome."

Jeez, Astra.

How eloquent.

Hades looked at me.

I looked back, my stomach a nervous bowl of butterflies.

The longer I sat with this, the more off-kilter I felt.

I mean, a year ago, I spent hours with Apollo in Palm Beach, and I never had a clue he could be my father. (Okay, granted, the dude had a boyfriend, so how would I have guessed he had an affair with my mother?) He came to my house! He attended the Arden Christmas party! How did I miss it? "Why didn't he tell me?" I whispered.

"Apollo, Poseidon, and Hermes swore not to tell any of you anything. In ancient Greek culture, swearing an oath was essentially a three-way contract between you, the person you were promising, and the gods," Hades explained. "Between the gods and from the gods, oaths are a serious commitment. Everyone honored it and trusted Minerva and Athena to handle you all. That...changed when you returned from the military. All of us felt a need to take a greater interest in all of you."

Great.

When I got home, I scared four gods about the damage the four of us could do together, so they made oaths and promised to spy on us for the rest of our lives.

Well, maybe.

"Why?" I asked.

"Because of Athena's gift."

Oh, right.

That.

"But you didn't promise or oath or whatever,

right? So that's why Mom only blocked you from all of us?"

"Yes, I can only assume so." He shook his head.

I had to stop myself from laughing at her naivety. If the gods—our dads—cared about talking to us, they would've found a way. They had immense power and creativity honed over thousands of years at their disposal—Mom was the one that told me that. My mother's hubris at thinking she could fool them and win was almost funny.

Almost.

If the myths tried to teach anything, it was that eventually karma would catch up to you. As that old Casablanca line goes: Maybe not today. Maybe not tomorrow, but soon and for the rest of your life.

Or, well, death, in her case.

"Why does Ayla have two major powers, and the rest of us have only one? If we're all demigods."

"Ah, yes, that," Hades said, his eyes taking on a faraway look. "Your mother asked me not to gift any offspring we might have with additional powers. It was a request she made to all her partners."

I struggled not to shudder.

I knew of four.

I didn't want to know of any more.

"Why?"

"She wanted you all to have a level playing field and not be at a disadvantage or an advantage because of your birthright. But Ayla…"

He trailed off, and I waited patiently for him to continue.

"Ayla is my daughter," he said finally. "She is my daughter as well as your mother's. Nothing your mother could say or do or cast could change that. And when it came time for her birth, I could not deny her the gifts that were rightfully hers."

Well, thanks so much, Poseidon, Apollo, and Hermes.

Cowards.

As if he could see my thought, Hades added, "Your father respected your mother's request not to gift you with multiple powers, Astra. But he regretted it. Even though he did not gift you with a secondary power, you have many of his gifts." Hades's eyes glowed as he smiled at me. "Your calm nature, for one."

"Wait a minute. How do you know what I'm like and what I'm not like?"

Hades chuckled again and shook his head. "I know you better than you think, Astra. We've been watching you for years, monitoring you and your sisters. You're a strong woman, one who has always possessed the courage and tenacity to stand up for what she believes in. You may not be my biological daughter, but that doesn't mean I don't love you as if you were. You're my daughter's sister."

I was stunned by Hades' words and stared at him in disbelief. How could he possibly mean this? Anyone who has read the myths surrounding the Olympians will know that the Greek gods were known for being cruel and ruthless, rather than compassionate and kind.

I told him as much.

"Everything evolves, Astra," my grandmother said as she came around the stacks to stand with us. She didn't ask Hades' permission to join our conversation.

She didn't seem to need it.

"Values, ethics. They all change with time. The Olympians are no different. We've had to adapt to the changing world around us, just like everyone else."

"But you're still the same gods that people have been worshipping for thousands of years," I protested. "My mother's practices weren't much different from—"

"Yes, they were." Hades shook his head. "Not as different as they should have been, I'll grant you that. But we're different now. This place is different now. We've changed just as the world has changed. And we will continue to change as time goes on. Just as you will change, Astra. As we all will change."

I nodded my head in response.

"We're not the same witches we once were, either, my dear," my grandmother agreed. "We've changed and evolved, just as humans have. We're not perfect, by any means, but we try to live by a code of ethics and values that is more in line with what the world expects. What humans strive for."

"This speech from you both would be a lot more believable if we hadn't been kidnapped by Althea's father—with the help of my father—and drug down here to the underworld." I told Hades. "Your wife didn't seem all that interested in our well being, if you want to know the truth." I raised my eyebrow. "Who then killed my boyfriend and mother."

"Some things, like ethics and morality, evolve over time, Astra," my grandmother explained.

"Some things, like the balance of the universe and the desire of women to get revenge on those that wronged them, do not," Hades added with a chuckle.

Okay, you misogynistic—

"H-hello." Ayla peaked around the corner shyly.

I smiled. "Hey, Ayla."

She slowly stepped out from behind the bookshelf, her eyes cast down at the floor as she wrung her hands nervously. "Hades…" Ayla whispered as she looked up at him. "I, um…I…"

"Yes, my child?" Hades reached out and touched Ayla's cheek gently with his hand.

I could see the resemblance between her and the god of the underworld immediately. They had the same shaped face and the same intense eyes. Ayla's wild mass of black ringlets resembled the deep blue-black of Hades long, wavy locks.

I moved to leave and give them privacy, but Ayla flashed a piercing look my way and shook her head, lips poised in a forced smile. "Stay," she whispered. "Please."

I stayed.

Hades and Ayla looked at each other in silence for what felt like forever. I could feel the tension between them, thick and electric in the air.

Finally, Ayla stepped forward and threw her arms around Hades in a tight hug. "Thank you for my gifts," she whispered. "Thank you for telling me." She paused, turning her head so it was buried in Hades' chest. "Dad."

The god of the dead and the king of the underworld smiled with visible relief.

Hades hugged her back just as tightly and patted her head gently. "You are very welcome, my child," he whispered. Hades patted her back soothingly as she trembled against him.

CHAPTER SIXTEEN

*E*veryone got answers. Past secrets were uncovered and brought out into the... well, not sunlight, but close enough, I guess. That's not why we're here...or maybe it was. Maybe this is what we needed. Maybe this is what we all needed. I don't know.

And yet we still didn't know who brought us here. It was as if the person who had orchestrated this wanted us to have closure, but at the same time, wanted us to keep wondering.

Jason gazed at me with concern. "What are you thinking?" he asked me. "You have that very 'Astra' look on your face. That expression that almost always signals our date is about to turn into a hunt for clues."

Gosh.

What a rosy view of our time together.

I frowned at him. "Sorry I was that bad of a date."

His eyes widened, and he looked agonized that I would say that. "It's not like that at all," he told me gently. "Astra, I had so much fun with you."

"Yep." Sure he did.

So much so that death looked fun.

"I mean it! I got to see parts of this world most human beings never get to see. I mean, look at me." He held his arms out wide. "I'm in a Greek god's library with an eternity to read every book. I mean, how many people get to do something like this?"

Nerd.

I might be annoyed, but I still didn't have the heart to tell him only Ayla could read anything in this room. He'd discover soon enough.

I winced a little as I studied him, taking in the sturdy cheekbones and full lips of his face and the way his sun-kissed hair was always mussed like he had been running. My eyes watered again as I realized how much I would miss him.

"I swear, Jason, your glass is always half full."

He grinned at me. "It's because I choose to see

the good in people and situations. And you, Astra, are one of the good things in my life. Well, you were. I mean, if I were still alive, you would be. But I'm not." Jason laughed. "It's going to take me a bit to get used to being dead."

I sighed and turned away from him, not wanting him to see the tears that threatened to fall. Instead, I watched my sisters and my mother as they argued on the other side of the room under the watchful eyes of three wolves and a god of the underworld.

"Astra, what is it?" Jason asked, his voice filled with unease. "What's wrong?"

I shook my head, not trusting myself to speak.

"Please tell me," he implored.

I shook my head, fighting back the tears. "It's nothing," I said, trying to keep my voice from trembling. "I'm just happy that everyone has got the answers they've been looking for."

Okay, we weren't looking, but—

"But not you," Jason said, his brow furrowed in concern. "What is it you're still looking for?"

Staring at the swirling mists of the underworld that lined the corners of the room, I sighed. "I feel like this is why we were here, somehow," I told him. "But there's something more out there. Something that we're still missing."

"Well, if you think we're missing something, then we're definitely missing something," he said, coming up behind me and putting his arms around my waist. "Hit me. Tell me what's troubling you, what clues are nagging the back of your mind."

Oh, gods.

Seriously?

We stood there like that for a long moment, neither of us speaking. I realized as we stood there that had Jason Bishop been this affectionate, this sure of himself, and this confident in his sexy-man prowess while he was alive?

Well, I likely would already be married with kids.

I took a deep breath and turned back to face him. "Okay, so here's the thing. Before we got down here, a couple of things happened. One? That stupid toy soldier that was supposedly from Athena, right? The one that claimed Archie needed to be tested." I held up my stock still, silent owl on my right arm.

Jason's brow furrowed with worry and he nodded for me to continue.

"The other thing is that Ami pulled out a glowing star card for the owl," I said, gesturing toward my sisters. "That card glowing for someone means that Athena, the goddess, demands that I go stop a death because she doesn't agree with it. It's not someone just at risk, though we say that for expediency, I guess. It's someone destined to die, and I have to prevent that."

"So, you think that's what we're missing?" Jason asked. "The death that Athena wants prevented?"

"No, not—look, the toy soldier was obviously just a trick to get us down here. I was the only one that touched it, and yet all of my sisters got dragged down here with me," I told him. "Apollo, Poseidon, and Hades are obviously involved because we've met them. The only person we haven't seen yet in this weird family drama is Hermes." I thought about Ace. "And I'm not all that sure about that."

"That you haven't seen him?"

I nodded.

Jason was silent for a long moment, his brow furrowed in thought. "You may be onto something there, Astra," he said finally as he looked at Archie. "But wouldn't your owl say something? He's supposed to be a connection to Athena, right?"

I looked at Archie. The bird hadn't said a word or flung an insult since he and Hades had their brief exchange with one another about Poseidon. "Why did Hades' statement about water versus the sea frighten you so much?"

Archie hooted.

Not helpful. It was like I suddenly had a regular owl.

"I don't know what's going on with him. Regardless, though, Athena's supposed actions just don't fit. If the goddess wanted us to know who our fathers were, wouldn't she just demand that Mom tell us? Why go through all this?"

"You're asking the wrong person, love," Jason said with a shrug. "I don't know how gods and goddesses think. Maybe this is all some grand test that you have to pass in order to prove yourselves worthy of whatever it is she wants you to do. Or maybe we need to talk to Hades? Maybe he can shed some light on this for us."

I frowned. "That seems awfully convoluted for Athena," I said. "She's not known for being subtle or playing games like that. She's usually pretty straightforward." I looked at Archie, and he shrugged. "No, I think there's something else going on here. Something that we're not seeing."

* * *

MY MIND RACED as I tried to puzzle out the strange events that had led me to this moment. Who was ultimately behind this? Was Athena involved in any of it, and if she was, what did that mean for Athena's coven? My powers? Archie? And why wasn't Archie talking?

As I continued to think about it, an idea formed in my mind. Maybe this was all part of some elaborate scheme by Hades—the god of the underworld—to gain power over Athena and her followers. After all, her high priestess kept him from his kid. This was his realm.

I looked at Archie once more, wondering if he might have some insight into this whole situation. But instead of offering me any advice or guidance, he simply hooted quietly once more and stared back at me with his large, unblinking eyes.

I was frustrated by his silence and his apparent lack of interest in our predicament. Reaching down, I grabbed a handful of wolf fur. "Please tell me you see something I don't."

"I see a lot that you don't," Lothian responded. "I'm a wolf. My eyes are retroreflective."

I stared down at him.

"That means light passing through the retina is reflected back into my eye," he responded calmly.

I knew what retroreflective meant, but I wasn't sure how that applied to the current situation. "What does that have to do with anything?"

"It means I can see in the dark," Lothian said matter-of-factly. "And I can see things you can't. Hence my answer."

Between Archie and Lothian, I was well and truly ready to jump into the nearest ravine. How bad could Tartarus really be?

I bet they didn't have snarky paranormal animals there.

"I know you can," I thought with a forced calm. Of course he could. He was a wolf. But that didn't help me solve the mystery of what was going on here. "But that's not what I mean, and you know it. In this situation, have you spotted anything that might tell me who's ultimately behind all this?"

He stared at me with an expression that clearly said he was trying to decide whether to answer. Finally, he spoke. "I don't know. But what I do know? Athena's the goddess of war, Astra. You all seem very focused on her wisdom. You talk about it all the time. You and your family never seem to remember her warfare." Lothian huffed toward my sisters and mother, still bickering in a circle. "Well, maybe not your mother. Her high priestess had four children from other gods." He turned back to me. "My question would be why. That seems awfully deliberate, don't you think?"

A voice interrupted the two of us, and it scared me so badly I nearly jumped out of my skin. "Because Athena wished to strike at the other gods through their children if the need arose."

I turned my head. And there he was, the god Apollo, his kind face framed by those legendary golden curls. Poseidon had apparently slipped into the room with him, and as everyone noticed, all the bickering fell silent.

"Dad," I said flatly.

Apollo grinned at me, his handsome face alight with joy. He moved toward me, arms outstretched in a gesture of pure affection. But I held my hand up and held my ground, refusing to let him get any closer.

He stopped. "You're angry with me."

Gosh, dude, you think?

What I think is I lost it. Just a little.

"Of course I am!" I said, my voice trembling with emotion. "You didn't tell me when we met a year ago. You didn't tell me you were my father. You lied to my face! How would you feel?"

My sisters looked surprised at my outburst, and my mother looked pained.

Apollo flinched as if I had physically struck him and stepped back. "I'm sorry, Astra. I wanted to, but Minerva and Athena made me swear an oath that I would not reveal my identity to you. I'm sorry. I didn't mean to keep it from you. It's just...it's complicated. It took a while to—"

I snorted. "Complicated? You're a god. You should be able to handle anything, right? Are you telling me you can handle anything except my mother?"

Poseidon stepped forward then, his hand resting on Apollo's shoulder in a comforting gesture. "As he said, it's not that simple, Astra. We are only as powerful as the followers that we have, even between the gods of Olympus."

"Until the four of us agreed to join together," Hades explained, standing next to Apollo and

Poseidon, "no single one of us could break the oath without consequences."

"You didn't have an oath," Ayla said to her father.

"And it was a good thing that he didn't," Apollo said, smiling at Ayla warmly. "Without Hades' refusal to become bound as we were, this may never have worked." Apollo reached out and shook his hand. "I owe you a debt of gratitude."

So it was them?

Just them.

No…that didn't seem right.

"You owe me more than that," Hades reminded him.

"Yes, well, we can discuss that later." Apollo turned back to me, and the smile faded from his face. "I'm sorry, Astra. I really am. If it makes you feel any better, I've been trying to keep an eye on you from afar. Make sure you were okay."

I crossed my arms over my chest and glared at him. "You've been stalking me. Yeah, that makes me feel so much better."

Poseidon sighed. "You make it sound so sinister when you say it like that."

The god of water seemed to have an opinion about everything.

"Why tell us now?" I demanded. "What

difference does it make whether I know that you're my father? It changes nothing."

"It changes everything," Poseidon said quietly, speaking for my father once more. "You are the child of a god, Astra. All of you are. You have a responsibility to the world that mortals do not."

"Oh, here it comes," Althea muttered.

"You rolled in the sheets with our mother and now we have yet another responsibility? What responsibility?" I scoffed. "I don't even know what you're talking about, and not for nothing, gentlemen? We barely know you."

Hades' eyes narrowed at me with intent as he spoke. "We will teach you," Hades said. "All of us."

All the gods suddenly working together was a little weird.

Father's Rights, Olympian-style.

"You realize we're all grown up already, don't you?" Ami spoke up, her eyes searching out the shadowed corners of the room for her—I guessed—divine father's appearance. "We can decide for ourselves whether to accept your fatherly wisdom." Ami crossed her arms. "Wisdom, by the way, we didn't solicit."

Poseidon frowned. "Yes, well, I'm not trying to impose my will on you."

Althea rolled her eyes and let out a loud sigh.

"That's good, because you wouldn't get very far, Pops," she told her father, her chin held high in defiance.

Poseidon clenched his jaw.

"You are all stronger than you realize," Poseidon said, his voice filled with conviction. "You will learn to harness these powers and use them for good. Together, we can do great things."

"If you choose," Apollo said.

"Yes," Hades agreed. "If you choose."

* * *

THE SURROUNDING air seemed to shimmer with energy as the three gods stepped forward. For a moment, I felt like I was soaring high above the earth, looking down at all of humanity with a sense of wonder and awe—

—but then it faded away as quickly as it had come as Persephone shimmered between us and our three fathers. She stared at the gods with a stern expression on her beautiful face, her eyes flashing with power. Ace stood quietly beside her.

"You may think you are ready for this," she said, her voice echoing through the room like a clap of thunder. "But you are not yet prepared for what is coming."

"Um. Excuse me?" Ayla asked. "What's coming?"

Hades frowned at his wife. "Persephone, don't scare the girls—"

"The girls?" The goddess laughed a rich laugh. "I wasn't talking to them. I was talking to you three."

The gods exchanged nervous glances as Persephone continued staring at them with fierce intensity.

"Plot twist, I guess," Ayla whispered.

I elbowed her in the side.

"Who is that again?" Ami asked as she pointed at Persephone. "I forgot."

The goddess whirled on my mother. "That. That right there. Before we go any further, you will remove every binding, blockage, or brainwashing that you have wrapped these girls in."

No one moved.

"Do it. Now."

Persephone's words were like a physical blow, and all the air seemed to be sucked out of the room, but my mother withstood it and stared back at the goddess in disbelief.

"No offense intended, goddess, but you can't just come in here and demand that I undo all the magic I've fortified them with," my mother protested. "I don't serve you, and they are my daughters."

"I am not just some random goddess," Persephone said, her voice filled with power. "I am the queen of the underworld, and you belong to my realm now. They are adults, or nearly so even in your world. You will do as I say."

"I will not."

Persephone's eyes narrowed. "I can see it, you know. The way you've been tampering with their memories, their very thoughts. It stops now." Persephone stepped forward, her power crackling around her like a storm. "Minerva? I warn you. Do. Not. Test. Me."

"Mom, what is she talking about?" Ami asked.

My mother looked back at Ami, sighed, and then nodded. "Very well," she said. "But I must warn you, girls. Once these bindings are removed, there is no telling what could happen. You could be in danger."

"We can handle it," Althea said confidently.

"Yeah, haven't you heard? We're demigods," Ayla deadpanned.

My mother nodded and chanted under her breath. A bright light surrounded us, and I felt a sudden jolt as the bindings were removed. It was like being unplugged from an electrical socket, and I felt disoriented as memories flooded back into my mind.

"Good." Persephone turned to the four of us. "Now, let's start from the beginning, shall we?"

CHAPTER SEVENTEEN

As the goddess stepped toward us, a long mahogany table stretched across the room out of thin air, the chairs immediately pulled back by an invisible force. After a moment of hesitation, everyone slowly made their way toward one—even the gods.

My mother took her seat at the head of the table first, followed by Althea, and then Ayla, and finally Ami, who sat to one side. I joined them, Archie still silent on my shoulder. I looked around, but my grandmother was nowhere to be found.

Our fathers and Ace sat across from us— Apollo across from me, Ace across from Ami, Hades opposite Ayla, and an annoyed Poseidon across from Althea. Cerberus scurried to Ayla's feet, and each of the wolves lay on the stone floor behind us.

Poseidon and Hades immediately began discussing something quietly as Jason, seeing only one seat available and two people standing, wandered away to peruse the library's stacks of books.

Persephone paused for a moment, appraising the table. With a nod, she took the free seat at the head. The one opposite my mother.

The table was dressed in yellow linen and decorated with bouquets of pink tulips. Once we'd all settled, four black candles appeared in the center of the table. Persephone lit them, and the small flames flared.

"So, let's start with introductions that have not yet formally been made," Persephone said, her smile warm and sweet. "I am Persephone, goddess of springtime, plants and flowers, and the queen of the underworld."

I remembered her myths and history. I knew her. I remembered everything now. It was as if waves crashed in my head, depositing layers of submerged information churned up from the depths by a violent sea storm.

The goddess gestured toward Ace. "I sense

some of you have guessed, but he should be introduced more formally. This is Hermes, god of travelers, athletes, thieves, the messenger of the gods, and the guide of the souls of the dead to the underworld." She looked at Ami. "He is your father."

"He must have trouble fitting that on a business card," Althea murmured.

"Apologies for the deception," he said with a bow of his head. "But it's kind of my thing."

"What's your thing?" I asked.

"I am the god of guile in its many aspects. Those aspects include deception." Ace slowly morphed into Hermes, his black clothes becoming that of a simple green tunic. The symbol of the caduceus—a staff with two snakes intertwining around it—appeared on his shirt. He nodded at Ami, who looked horrified.

"You're my dad?" Ami asked.

Ace nodded. "I am."

"Wow," Ami whispered.

"Yes, Ami. You are a daughter of Hermes," Persephone said, her voice ringing with satisfaction. She seemed pleased as she sat across from my mother, her hair cascading over her shoulders, glinting lightly as it caught the light from the flickering flames. "The sweet, demure little girl who we all watched grow up into a strong young woman."

Althea stifled a chuckle. "Ami. Born from the blood of the god of deception." She raised an eyebrow. "Yeah, that just doesn't feel right to me."

"What do you mean? How could you watch me?" Ami asked, anger in her voice.

"Ignore them. They claim to have seen far more than they could have," my mother told Althea, snorting contemptuously and folding her arms. "The wards that I set on you girls and the house—"

"Minerva, is this truly something you want to brag about?" Persephone asked, interrupting. Her voice dripped with skepticism.

My mother stared at Persephone, her expression determined and unwavering. "You have no right to pass judgment on me for what I've done or what I didn't do," she said, her voice unwavering. "This is a family issue, Persephone. While I'll admit I may have gotten carried away with protecting the girls from your family's 'Real Gods of Central Florida' power plays and dramas, they are still my daughters. I never harmed them."

"And what about Astra?" she said, her voice echoing through the room like a clap of thunder.

"You stick to your argument like a lifeline, even though you must know it to be false."

My mother's nostrils flared as she took in a breath and wrinkled her forehead. She waved her arms and opened her mouth to speak, but nothing came out. Mom looked surprised. Even a little concerned.

"When you and Athena decided to use her to hold Astraea's power, did you tell her what that meant?" Persephone asked with a smile too warm and too sweet.

"What are you talking about?" my mother asked Persephone, her voice trembling slightly. "Is that why you brought all of us here? Not because I diddled your husband, but because of Astra?"

Althea leaned over to me and whispered, "This is starting to look a little like your fault." She pet my shaking owl. "I'm just saying."

I wanted to tell Althea to shut up, but, well…

She wasn't wrong.

"Did you tell her what happened before?" Persephone hissed at my mother, her eyes growing wide and flashing with the power of her anger. "Asclepius, son of Apollo and peerless healer throughout all time? A skilled physician so remarkable that he even had a cure for death?"

My mother bristled at this statement but said nothing as Persephone continued speaking, and the air in the room seemed to crackle with energy.

"—a thwarting of destiny, you'll remember, that infuriated Zeus. Or do you remember?" Persephone asked, her beautiful face contorted into a mask of fury. "Where did you learn to block truths from your daughters' minds, Minerva? Gods like Athena interfere with humans to satisfy their own desires, don't they? Did you think you would be different?"

My mother, devoted high priestess of Athena, sat with a look of shock and confusion on her face.

"When you and Athena concocted your seduction plan to bear demigod children in some insane plot to challenge the other gods, we dismissed your scheme." Her eyes burned with anger. "After all, demigod children cover the face of the earth. They are in all continents, and all countries."

"Even Antarctica?" Ayla asked, surprised.

"Yes. I have a daughter there studying sea level rise," Poseidon told her. "Most demigods live quiet lives, free of the world's dangers. Their names are unknown to the public, but they quietly bear witness to our humanity."

"But you, Minerva, were so sure that your bedchamber would produce higher quality children, weren't you?" Persephone said.

Okay, yuck.

"And you were not entirely wrong. But once Astra was elevated to goddess—"

"Hey, ho, wait a sec, now," I said, jumping up out of my seat. "I'm not some goddess. Hell, most days—if we're being entirely honest here—I'm barely a witch."

"You mortals and your ignorance," Persephone's voice was oddly sweet and bitter. "The world of the gods is not one you can understand."

"Awesome. Thanks for clearing that up," I said, visibly annoyed. "If that's the case, can we leave?"

"We didn't think that we would need to spell this out for you." Persephone glared at me, but I was unfazed. "Yet it appears that we must. We all were surprised when Astraea's power was given to you, but what concerned us even more was Athena's charge that you stop deaths that were destined by the Fates."

"It was Asclepius all over again," Apollo said

sadly. My father had a mournful look in his eyes. "Perhaps a different power, and a unique form of that energy, but if Zeus came down off his mountain or picked his head up to notice what you were doing, I feared you would be killed for it."

Covering his mouth with one hand and looking at my mother from over his manicured fingernails, Hermes admitted, "We tried to explain this to your mother, but she ignored us."

"You're just making this up." Ayla said, standing up with me. "You're trying to scare us." She pointed. "I mean, you already killed our mother and Jason. You're not exactly people with our best interests at heart. Why should we believe anything you say?"

The silence stretched out for what felt like an eternity.

* * *

My mother finally broke the noiseless library's stillness.

"Hermes is speaking the truth. For once." She reclined in her chair and brushed away a lock of gray hair from her forehead. There was hopeless resignation on her face. "Athena assured me they were bluffing. That Zeus—"

Persephone's voice was low and raspy as she said, "You and Athena thought you had enough blocks and mind wipes and brainwashing that your daughters would stand with Athena against the other gods."

'No,' my mother started, 'I—'

"You hoped you'd turned your daughters into weapons to be used against us."

My mother's jaw hung low, her eyes wide. Her mouth worked, groping for words. Finally, she simply shook her head, denying what Persephone was saying.

"You lie." Persephone's gaze was fastened on my mother, judging, distrustful.

"Okay, enough," I said. "Give her a break. Let her talk."

Persephone peered at me, as if gauging me.

"It was never a weapon," my mother said in a hushed voice. "I would never use my children as weapons. That's abhorrent—" Her voice broke. She looked down and shook her head. "I cared about each one of these gods. It wasn't a plot. My affairs were not plots. As a High Priestess of an American Olympian, why wouldn't I want demigod children?"

"You accepted Astraea's power from Athena for Astra before she ever had the choice,"

Persephone told my mother, her voice low and menacing, "and then you tried to control what she could do with that power."

"I did not," my mother said, weariness and resignation layering her voice. "You don't understand. It wasn't a weapon." Her voice was odd; a low-pitched breathy tone unlike her usual assertive voice. "Athena offered a way for Astra to help people once the military fell apart."

"You—" Persephone began, but she stopped speaking and cocked her head to the side. "Ugh. You have no idea what you've done. Petty mortal dramatic games. Your service to Athena allows you to be led around by her like a dog on a leash."

"Hey, watch how you talk to my mother," I snapped.

"Persephone—" my father began, but the goddess held up her hand.

"No!" she retorted. "She birthed four children for Athena's resentment against the rest of us. Whether or not she knew it was for that means nothing."

"Ignorance is an excuse when someone is brainwashed, Persephone," Apollo told her. "Perhaps Minerva really didn't know—"

"Really?" Persephone said, radiating victimized trauma and accusation all at the same time. "Am I getting out of here now because I didn't know the consequences of eating the pomegranate seed?"

Hades rolled his eyes as if he'd heard this complaint a thousand times, and was resigned to hear it a thousand more. "Here we go."

"She risked Zeus's wrath against her own daughter, your daughter. We had to plot just for these girls to know who their fathers were!" Persephone looked at Mom with a look of such disgust I thought the goddess might throw a lightning bolt and burn her to a pile of ashes on the spot.

"You can say whatever you want about my naivete, about my ignorance, about how Athena used me. What you can't say is that I meant to hurt these girls. I love my daughters," my mother said, shaking her head in denial. "A concept you, I'm sure, can't even fathom. After all these years, you still don't understand mortals at all, do you?"

Persephone stood up ready to unleash her fury on my mother.

"We're getting nowhere," I said, interrupting her continued attack. "Whatever my mother did or didn't do, though, is between us and her. Maybe them and her," I said, looking at Apollo and the other dad gods. "But it doesn't concern you. So, let's get to what does—what is it you want from us?"

"Your mother's ignorant mistakes have put you in danger," Persephone said, an edge of anger in her voice. "You are in danger. If Zeus ever finds out what you have been doing—"

"Yup. You already said that. Look, not for nothing and it's sure not me trying to excuse my choices, but I was told I had to run around doing Athena's bidding," I said as I finally sat back down in my chair. "If Zeus found out, I'd tell him that."

"You had a choice," Persephone said. "When you have a choice, you are responsible."

"Fine, I'm responsible," I said with a shrug, looking at Persephone and then at my mother. "My mother is responsible for whatever she did. I'm responsible for what I did. Archie is responsible for what he did." The owl hid his head in my shoulder. "It's pretty simple, and I don't think we need an all-hands-on-deck family meeting to discuss it." I leaned forward, my eyes fixated on Persephone. "I have to tell you—I'm tiring of this whole thing."

"Me, too," Althea agreed. "I still don't know why we're here, and I don't know what you want from us. If you wanted us to know our fathers, okay. Great. Done. What else?"

Apollo and Hades looked at each other.

"What?" I asked suspiciously. "What's that look?"

"It's nothing. I don't want to see this escalate any further," Apollo said, and the room's energy seemed to shift, as if the air had suddenly become thicker and more intense. "But I don't see a way around it."

Crap.

What did I do now?

Apollo shifted in his seat, sighed, and then leaned forward. "What we really wanted to tell you all, aside from your parentage, is that Athena cannot take the power from you, Astra." Apollo glanced at Archie. "Any more than she could take Archibald back."

I pulled my owl closer. "Archimedes. His name is Archimedes."

"Whatever his name," the god smiled. "A gift like this once given is given. It cannot be taken back. Not even by a god."

A look of incredulity came over my mother's face. She cast her eyes down, and her voice broke as she spoke. "No," she whispered. "You're lying—"

"We are not, Minerva. Between the two of us,"

Apollo said with a dip of his head, "I am not the one prone to hiding the truth."

Mom blushed red.

"You were born of a choice, Astra," Persephone said, her voice growing in intensity. "And you were given powers of your own choosing. So you are responsible for the good and the bad that has come and will come of these powers. You may have been told you were required to be a mindless follower, but you never have been."

"I was told to do it for the good of the world," Mom said, her voice breaking with emotion. "For the good of our daughters."

"No, you were told to do it for the good of Athena," Persephone said, shaking her head. "You were told to do it because Athena wanted to do it. Not because it was good for the world. And in doing it, your daughters were placed in grave danger."

"Again, folks, I didn't know." I said. "I didn't know I had a choice, and I didn't know Zeus was all uptight about changing people's fate and all. Got it. Hear you. I—"

"How could you know?" Persephone asked, and she was looking at me and my mother, her eyes hard and angry. "Only your mother knew.

And if she told you, she and Athena would lose control of you. You didn't know, but your mother knew."

Man, Persephone just didn't stop, did she?

"But I didn't, not all of it," Mom said, her words coming out in a stilted and halting fashion. "I was—"

"You knew enough," Persephone said, her voice rising. "You were afraid of what Athena would say if you refused. Afraid of thinking for yourself. Afraid of realizing your goddess wasn't perfect. So you ignored the signs."

"No," Mom repeated. "I'm telling you. I didn't know."

"You knew," Persephone said adamantly.

"Okay, this is all old news, and again, stop pounding on my mother with an accusation hammer. You already killed her. How much more do you want from her? How vindictive do you need to be?" I asked. "Let me know so we can set aside exactly the amount of time you need to torture a mortal far weaker than you."

Persephone fell silent.

I looked at my mother. "She is right, though, Mom. You kept things from me."

Ami nodded, agreeing. "You kept things from all of us. And it got you and Jason killed."

"I am…sorry. I am responsible for the consequences of my own actions," my mother said, her voice trembling. "But I am not responsible for Athena's actions or her lies of omission. I really was trying to keep you girls safe," Mom said, looking at Ami and me.

"I know, Mom," I said, my voice cracking.

What a mess.

"I am so sorry I couldn't protect us from her," Mom said, looking at Persephone. "You can see why I tried so hard to block her."

"So far, the only person she's killed is you," Althea deadpanned. "And it kinda sounds like she had a bunch of reasons for that, Mom."

"Althea! She killed Jason," Ayla reminded her.

"Oh, shoot. Right."

"I did not," Persephone disagreed. "Ami chose who would come to take her place. They were the first two people that she thought of once she agreed to the switch. I took the life of no one."

"Talk about splitting hairs. You wanted someone to eat the popcorn," I accused.

"True. I did," Persephone said nodding her head.

"She knew one of you girls would think of me," my mother said, standing up in the chair, her face pale in the darkness. "My being here is not,

I'm guessing, part of an intricate plot. My death is just that woman's revenge on me."

"You are responsible for the consequences of your actions, High Priestess," Persephone said while staring at my mother as if she was a bug the goddess had to squash. "You betrayed the sisterhood, as did Athena. But you are wrong, Minerva, that your death is just revenge. With your death ends their oath," Persephone gestured toward our fathers, "to you."

"So now, instead of just Athena using us, those four can use us instead," Althea whispered. "Awesome."

"It also ends Athena's covenstead temple in the United States," Apollo added. "You did not choose a successor. You took too much time deciding between Astra and Ami, and now neither will serve in your place."

"And no one else will, either," Persephone said.

"Which means Athena has lost the gains she made over the rest of us, and she will no longer use Ami and Astra to undo what destiny and the Fates have already decided," Hades said, and he dipped his head toward my father. "Apollo's daughter now knows she is beholden to only herself."

"Okay, great. Awesome." I looked around. "I still feel like we're going in circles."

"You are," Hermes said with a smile. "But that is the nature of this place. It is designed to confuse and confound. I think it is time we all take our leave." Hermes looked at Apollo and Poseidon. "If you are ready for me to return you."

They nodded.

"I agree," Persephone said, and she held out her hand to Hades. "We have done as much as we can for now."

For now?

What the hell did that mean?

"It sounds like you all have a lot to process," Hermes said. "I will take you all back home, and we can talk more later."

Ami looked stricken. "Wait a minute—"

IN AN ABRUPT INSTANT before Ami could finish her thought, we were back home, and I was lying on my bed, staring at the ceiling. So much had happened in such a short amount of time—at least I hoped we were gone for a short amount of time—and I still didn't feel like I had any answers.

Archie gasped and flapped his wings. "Finally!"

"What the hell happened to you?"

"Hades," he muttered to himself, some of his frustration and anger clearly on display. "He decided my commentary wouldn't be helpful during their dog and pony show, so he removed my ability to talk."

Ami raced up the stairs to my attic bedroom. The room was sparsely decorated with simple furnishings and soothing earth tones. It seemed oddly gentle after a day in the underworld. "Hey, you okay? Is Archie back, too?"

"Yes, he's back and can talk again." I sighed. "And no, not really. I feel like I just got hit by a truck."

She came and sat on the edge of my bed. "Me, too. At least your new dad talked to you. Mine barely looked at me the whole time." Ami rubbed her eyes. "Time to think about that later. What do you think is going to happen now?"

I shrugged. "I don't know. But whatever it is, we'll face it together."

CHAPTER EIGHTEEN

Traveling from the underworld back to the incense-perfumed home of my family in the blink of an eye, I tried to focus on the present.

I was relieved that all three of my sisters returned safely, though Ayla brought home an English Bulldog and Althea's snowy white owl Lily had transformed into a crow the color of midnight. We wrapped our arms around each other, four distinct branches of a single family vine (now with animals perched above and below.)

"We're going to be there for each other, okay?" I said firmly. "No more fighting, no more bickering. We are a team now. The Four Musketeers. One for all and all for one."

"One for all and all for one," they repeated.

A faint glow of electric energy crackled around us. It filled the air with a buzzing, almost palpable intensity. Glowing tendrils of light flickered and danced, reflecting off the gleaming mirror in my room.

Before I could focus on it, it was gone.

Huh.

"Lily, you're a pretty bird and all, but I really wanted an owl," Althea grumbled, glancing at the sleek, dark bird with glossy feathers and beady black eyes. "Though I guess a crow is pretty cool."

Lily's head cocked back and forth as she watched my sister. Then the crow screeched loudly as if to agree.

"Oh, jeez. Seriously?" Archie muttered.

"Oh, jeez, oh, jeez, oh, jeez," Lily repeated.

Althea's shoulders slumped. "Mine can't talk like Archie? Seriously? Aw, man!"

Looking around at my sisters, I felt a mix of emotions—relief and gratitude, mostly. A fierce sense of pride and love for them. Let's face it— few people could go through what we had just been through and come out standing tall.

Despite all that, I couldn't help but feel a lingering sadness that we had lost so much.

"You think Hades gave me a dog for Christmas or something?" Ayla asked as she scratched the bulldog behind the ears. He—and it was most definitely a he—had a large white splotch on its chest and a wet, black nose. "He looks like Cerberus."

"I think he is Cerberus, Ayla!" Althea pointed to the tag on the dog's collar. "Look!"

The tag said CERBERUS HEAD #3.

"No way," Ayla whispered. "Cerberus? Is that you?"

The bulldog licked her face.

"Girls!" Aunt Gwennie's call rang up from my attic door. "Are you here? Are you back?" Before any of us could answer, she added, "Come downstairs!"

At the sound of my aunt's voice, I felt a sudden longing for the taste of my mother's cooking—my favorite Greek dishes, the familiar aromas of oregano and roasted lamb and lemon. In the underworld's aftermath, I felt an unexpected connection to the spirit of a holiday I never really valued before.

A holiday that could never be the same, now, without Mom.

Aunt Gwennie stood in the middle of the foyer, hands on her hips, face full of concern. "Are you girls all right?"

I nodded. "We're fine, Aunt Gwennie," I said.

Her eyes traveled over each of us. Convinced that we were okay, she gave each of us a long hug. "I'm so happy you're all home safe," she said. "After what happened to your mother and Jason…" She trailed off and blinked back tears. "Well, I just didn't know what to expect."

"The day wasn't exactly what we expected, either," I said. "So, you know what happened to Mom and Jason?"

Aunt Gwennie nodded. "I know. The authorities took their bodies a few hours ago." She shuddered. "They also took the party food under a suspicion there was poison or some such thing."

I had a nagging feeling of unease. Their deaths would probably perplex any coroner who came across them, and since my captain knew we were witches, I would have expected him to intervene. "The captain couldn't avoid—"

"Captain Harmon is probably going to fire you," Emma said entering the hall. The detective's face was stoic, her eyes downcast. "Jason's mother is furious with you. Well, you, your mother, witches in general, and if Forkbridge itself burned to the ground tomorrow, I don't think she'd bat an eye."

"Are they still here?"

"No, they left," another voice said.

"Who was that?" Ayla asked, confused.

A vaporous form appeared in front of us, surrounded by wispy tendrils of white smoke. The eerie figure was dimly lit, as if it were floating in the shadows. My other aunt's luminescent face turned toward me with a sad smile, her eyes full of compassion.

I was momentarily stunned. "Aunt Gertie?"

"I see her, too," Althea whispers.

"You two can see your aunt?" Aunt Gwennie asked, her face the picture of shock and surprise. "Is this some residual underworld thing?"

As we struggled to comprehend what had just occurred, Ami cleared her throat. "Look, it could be nothing, but did anyone else get all staticky when we were hugging upstairs?"

Althea's face was etched with confusion. "What do you mean, staticky?"

"Um, guys?" Ayla raised her hand. Between her fingers, tiny lightning bolts flashed. "This doesn't seem like a residual underworld thing to me."

Althea looked stunned. "Isn't that Astra's power?"

Aunt Gwennie was tense and rigid, and she appeared to be struggling to make sense of everything that was going on. "This is completely bizarre." She looks around. "No one?"

"One for all, and all for one," Althea murmured. "You don't think that group hug upstairs got...I don't know, misconstrued, do you?"

"What do you mean by 'misconstrued?'" Aunts Gwennie and Gertie spoke the same words from opposite sides of the mortal veil simultaneously.

"I have the hardest time following what's happening with you people," Emma spoke as the werewolves, now in human form, entered the hallway to join us.

Eddie wrapped his arm around Emma, drawing her closer to him. Lothian's gaze, I noticed, was intensely fixed on me. I also noticed his worried expression, as if he was troubled by what he saw.

Refocus, Astra.

"I think she's wondering if my Astraea power just spread all of our magical powers around to the group," I said quietly. "What we thought was a pep talk might have been taken as an incantation."

"Taken by who?" Emma asked.

"One for all and all for one? All four of you said that?" Aunt Gertie asked.

"At the same time," Ayla told her.

"While we all group hugged," Althea added.

"Oh, dear," Aunt Gwennie sighed. "Well, that's possible. It's quite nonspecific yet very meaningful. Sometimes that's how the most powerful magic happens."

"Nonspecific words that are meaningful?" Emma asks, surprised. "Jeez. That's not a recipe for disaster at all."

"One for all and all for one," Aunt Gwennie said. "It's possible. Definitely possible."

"Huh. I wonder…" Althea's head swiveled on her neck, and she grabbed an amethyst geode from the entryway table next to her. Clutching the geode tightly, her gaze fixed intently on the purple stone's cool, smooth surface. "You guys, I can see the party. I can psychometrize stuff."

"That's not a word," I told her.

"Yes, it is," she retorted. "Grab a dictionary and tell me I'm wrong. Now be quiet, I'm concentrating." Althea narrowed her eyes, her gaze intense and focused. "Oh, yeah, Emma's right. Mayor Lillian Thornton looks like she wants to kill someone."

Great.

That would probably be me.

* * *

WEAVING our way through the house, we picked our way through the remnants of the party (and the chaotic evacuation) until we arrived at the large living room. My mother had filled it with comfortable furniture arranged in a u-shape to facilitate discussion, but it had seen better days and happier chats.

As we sat down, our faces were tight with worry. In fact, the entire room was heavy with uncertainty, unusually quiet for a room with a bunch of chatterboxes.

"Well?" Aunt Gwennie asked.

We stared back.

"Okay, I'll start, then. The mayor said that with your mother's death, the treaty between the town of Cassandra and the witches of Forkbridge is over," Aunt Gwennie said. "And technically, I believe she's right. Your mother didn't choose a successor."

The werewolves exchanged worried glances, appearing anxious and uncertain. Lothian looked over to Eddie, as if seeking advice or direction.

"Later," Eddie murmured.

"She also demanded Captain Harmon fire you," Emma jumped in. "You're not a member of the union, so he can fire you for any reason." She put her feet up on the coffee table and exhaled in relief. "Oh, man, my feet are swollen. That feels better. Anyway, that reason includes the 'my girlfriend thinks her son's death is your fault' old chestnut."

Cerberus barked and scurried up next to Emma's legs.

"Oh, aren't you cute? Is that an English bulldog?" Emma asked. She scratched the dog behind his ears and cooed, "You're a good boy. Yes, you are." She looked up. "Where'd you guys get the dog?"

"The underworld," Ayla told her.

Emma froze. Cerberus whined and looked back at Emma with a pleading expression as she slowly, nervously withdrew her hand. "Um. He's cute."

"Yep, he is." Ayla slapped her thigh, and Cerberus hurried over for pets and scratches.

"Perhaps you should tell us what happened to you tonight, girls," Aunt Gwennie prompted. "All we know is what we saw here, and what little rumors Aunt Gertie could communicate after visiting the United States branch of the Greek underworld."

Eddie nearly choked. "The what now?"

I was glad he asked.

Because I had no idea what the hell Aunt Gwennie was talking about.

"There are many afterlifes," Aunt Gwennie said with a wave of her hand. "Your afterlife depends on where you lived your life, how you lived your life, what you believed. Many things."

"Like whether your sister binds your spirit to a tree and then banishes you from the sight of your family," my deceased Aunt Gertie complained, reminding us all of yet another one of my mother's machinations.

"We live here in the United States, and we follow the Greek gods, so our afterlife would be in the Greek underworld. Well, the North American version. Ayla, stop that, please," my living aunt told my sister distractedly as she sparked starlight from her fingers to entertain her dog. "All we need is for you to set the house on fire to round out this most unfortunate day."

"Sorry, Aunt Gwennie," Ayla grumbled as she dissipated her starlight back into her hand.

Cerberus whined.

"Anyway," Aunt Gwennie continued. "You were in the underworld. What happened?"

Sitting around the coffee table, my sisters and I exchanged nervous glances, each waiting for someone else to speak. I finally broke the silence, gradually outlining what I remembered in some version of a coherent narrative.

Eventually, my sisters jumped in as well.

Ayla explained Hades and his concerns, while Ami detailed what we saw in Asphodel Meadows. Althea described her surprising exchange with Hecate—and Ami wondered aloud why Hecate did not show up for the final meeting of gods and witches.

Lily, the crow, was silent the whole time.

So was Archie.

Our aunt listened attentively, her expression sad as she tentatively nursed her tea with honey. She never told us what part of our story she already knew. She didn't say a word until we were done.

For an hour and a half, we worked to make sense of our experiences, filling in each other's gaps as we went through it. We explained and repeated and talked until—at last—we breathed a collective sigh of relief.

We may not understand it, but at least

everyone knew now. It was the first step in figuring out what it all meant.

"So, wait a minute—that doctor we met last year was actually your father? The one with the beach front mansion in Palm Beach? Loxias, right? Holy—" Emma said, her eyes wide. She turned to Eddie. "You remember him, don't you? And Hermes, too. He brought that guy Godfrey."

Eddie nodded. "I knew him in Palm Beach. Nice man."

I snorted with disbelief.

"Wow. Okay, I feel less guilty about you getting fired from the department. I mean, since you're a goddess and all."

"I'm not a goddess," I told her.

"That's not what I just heard," Emma said, her expression bemused.

"Then you weren't listening."

"Well, even if you're not a goddess, you still have a super rich father. I bet you could easily get a guilt yacht out of him." She snaps. "Like that. He seemed the type to guilt-gift, didn't he?"

"Will you be serious? I'm not a goddess. I'm a..a demigod." I blushed. Even that sounded stupid.

"Well, we're all demigods, Astra" Ayla pointed out.

"Or is it demigoddess?" Althea asked.

Ami looked on silently, her expression glum.

"What's the difference?" Emma asked.

I shrugged. "I guess the big difference is that the gods are immortal. Demigods are not. Right?"

"Oh, man. So, you're not immortal?" Emma asked.

"Nope," I said with a shake of my head.

"Well, that sucks," she said. Emma looked thoughtful as she studied me. "You look like you've been through the ringer." Emma glanced around. "In fact, all of you do."

"It's been a hell of a day," Ami whispered.

"How are your Mom and Jason?"

"Jason?" I laughed. "Dude is all excited about being dead. Hades has a huge library. I swear, you would have thought the guy got a promotion at work—"

I stopped short. A knot formed in my stomach as I thought about Jason's students, and how they would feel upon hearing of his death.

"Astra," Aunt Gwennie said gently.

I took a deep breath, trying to steady myself. "Jason's students...they're going to be heartbroken. I'm sorry," I breathed. "I didn't mean—"

"Hey, it's okay," Emma said as she reached out

to pat my hand. "I fully understand. I'm sorry about your mother and Jason. I didn't mean to sound insensitive."

I felt a squeeze in my throat as the words left her lips, and tears threatened to fall. I blinked them back. "No, I'm just...I need some time to process everything."

"Oh, of course," Emma said.

We avoided discussing my mother, but I noticed Mom's usual seat on the couch remained unoccupied, as if we'd all decided to make room for her. It was strange, as if we were silently acknowledging the immense pain and sadness she left behind...

And, I reminded myself, that she had caused.

"I'll be fine," I said, my voice breaking.

"Can I talk to you?"

Lothian's eyes were an oddly vibrant sapphire color, and despite his serious demeanor, they sparkled with intense coy intelligence. Ugh, that steady gaze could be magnetic. Normally, I found the manipulative werewolf annoying, but on that particular day, his presence made me feel strangely calm and clear.

Weird.

"Of course," I said. I stood up, giving Emma a reassuring pat on the leg. "I'll be back in a few minutes."

"Take your time!" she smirked knowingly.

What she thought she knew?

I had no idea.

"First, I wanted to offer you my sympathies for losing your mother, and Jason," Lothian said as we stood alone together at the window of the ritual room, his expression as sincere as I'd ever seen it.

"Thank you."

"Second, an apology."

"For what?"

"I know I talked a lot of…well, you know." His eyes were downcast as he looked away for a moment.

It seemed like Lothian was struggling to find the words he wanted to say.

Which was…odd.

"We can talk later—"

"Look, I made fun of your relationship with Jason, and I used it to needle you. I had no right to do that. I shouldn't have done it. It was wrong, and I apologize. I'm sorry."

"No, you didn't have a right and no, you

shouldn't have done it," I answered. As if seized by a compulsion, I asked, "Why did you do it?"

I almost instantly regretted it.

Lothian's face was etched with remorse as he hesitated. Then he said, "It was a poorly told joke born from jealousy. I'm really sorry."

Jealous?

Jealous of what?

"Gods alive above and below, Astra. You really are the densest witch on the planet when it comes to men," Archie said in my mind.

I ignored Archie and prepared to ask—.

No.

I didn't want to ask anything.

I didn't want to know what Lothian was jealous of.

I didn't want to know about anyone other than Jason.

It was too soon, it was too much, it was…

No. Just no.

Even if Jason had let us go the moment he crossed over, I couldn't do it.

I wouldn't do it.

Finally, I said, "I can't."

Lothian gave me a curious look, and I felt my face heat. "Right, no, of course you can't. I don't know what I was thinking. Again—I'm sorry, I didn't mean to upset you. This wasn't even about this. I'm actually here to formally offer you my protection," he said. "Well, 'offer' may not exactly be the right word."

That dumped a bucket of cold water on my flashy hot embarrassed warmth.

"You're here to 'order' me to accept your protection?" I asked, my voice cool. "Is that what you're saying?"

Lothian's expression became more solemn, his eyes serious and thoughtful. "Look, I know I've been a jerk before, but I hope what happened in the underworld showed that I really can behave."

I raised an eyebrow.

"I just mean I'm not the kind of guy to push you into accepting my protection. Normally." His jaw was set in a firm line, and he seemed to weigh his words carefully.

"Okay. What would you call it?" I asked, my tone sharper than I intended. The emotions were still too raw, too close to the surface. "Get to it, Lothian, I haven't got all night." I glanced at the window. "Or morning."

The werewolf's expression shifted, his brow furrowing. "I know how this sounds. Damn it, I'm really screwing this up, aren't I? Look, I'm here," Lothian said, meeting my gaze, "to make sure you're safe. That's all. I would do it without being asked."

Uh huh.

"But you should know I've been told to do so. By your father."

"Apollo?"

He nodded.

"Fine. I'll bite. Make sure I'm safe from what?"

Lothian's features tightened. "I don't know. Honestly. Just...safe. And not just me. All the werewolves. You and your sisters."

I shrugged. "So? Tell him no."

He shook his head. "I can't. Neither can any of the other wolves. We're bound to protect you."

"Why on earth would you be bound to do what my absentee father tells you to do?" I asked, bewildered.

"He is the god of the wolves, and Eddie's decided we need to follow Apollo's directives."

I stared.

He waited for me to say something.

I didn't.

"Look, all I know is Apollo wants you all protected, and we're charged with protecting you. It's just that simple."

"Simple, huh?" I let out a long, heavy sigh,

feeling exasperated and annoyed. "It's not simple. I don't want your protection."

"I know," Lothian said. His expression was tense and uncertain. "I know you can take care of yourself."

I turned from him and looked out the window to find the sun peeking up over the horizon. "It's dawn," I murmured. The jubilant welcoming of the sun by the birds sounded like it was mocking me. "My father is a sun god, I think. Did you know that? Or something like that."

In one day, I gained a father and lost a mother.

Lost a boyfriend and gained a manipulative werewolf bodyguard.

At least the dog was cute.

I hoped he was house trained.

"I'm sorry," Lothian said quietly.

I turned back to him, my expression hard. "You keep saying that, but what exactly are you sorry for? That my mother is dead? Or that my boyfriend is dead? That my father is rich, immortal, and a big, fat liar? That the town of Cassandra and all its old lady psychics may be about to go to war with us? That I have to rely on the protection of werewolves and I have no choice in the matter? Or that I may have accidentally made my sisters and I the four most powerful witches on this or any other planet at a time of deep grief, which, you know, seems a little ill-advised?"

He met my gaze evenly, unflinching in the face of my anger. "All of it."

I looked away from him once more, back out the window, and sighed. I didn't want his pity, but I couldn't deny that his words touched me.

"Thank you," I muttered grudgingly. "You should be. This all sucks."

"I know." Lothian exhaled. "So…does that mean you accept our protection?"

I considered for a moment, then nodded. "Yes. For now."

"Good." His features tightened again as he seemed to become more focused and determined. "If you ever need anything…anything at all, please call me. I know we got off on the wrong foot, but I promise you, I will do everything in my power to help you."

I nodded, not trusting myself to speak.

"And Astra…I am sorry for what you're going through. And I'm sorry that I can't do more to help you. But I promise, we will protect you. All of you."

I nodded once more, still not trusting myself to speak.

The werewolf reached out and squeezed my shoulder before turning and walking out of the room so I could burst into tears without a witness to my humiliating mental breakdown.

Everything in my life—everything—had just changed.

All the rules, all the things I counted on.

Again.

My powers, my family, my role in life.

It was all different in an instant.

Once more, I was starting over.

"I hope this time will be the last time," I whispered.

"It will be."

CHAPTER NINETEEN

I whirled like a dervish in response to a familiar voice that seemed to emanate from thin air.

"Who's there?" I asked, my body tense.

"Forget me already?"

As I turned, I came face to face with an ethereal image of Jason, his face lit up with a warm smile. He seemed to exude a sense of quiet joy, as though he knew something that I didn't.

Oh, boy.

The words echo through my mind, tinged with a sense of dread. With Ayla's death speaker power, I'll be able to see my ghost boyfriend just walk into the shower, hover in while I bathed or changed or—

"Jason Bishop, you've got to be kidding," I said. "I was fine with you floating around all ghost-like when I couldn't see you, but now I'm going to be afraid to go to the bathroom!"

Jason laughed. "Don't worry. I'm not here to spy on you."

"Okay," I said, my tone clearly suspicious of his claim.

"I just wanted to tell you that everything will be okay. You'll all figure out your powers, you'll learn to work together, and you'll come out of this better than you were. Trust me, Astra. Everything will eventually be okay."

I wanted to be angry at him for poofing into the ritual room like a spy, but I couldn't be angry at him.

He was Jason, after all.

I could never be angry with Jason.

I let out a shaky breath, feeling my frustration and grief slipping away. "Let's hope you're right."

"And I promise to respect your privacy. We can come up with some formal rules tomorrow after you get some sleep," he said with a grin. "But I wanted you to know I will always be here whenever you need me."

I felt my heart lighten slightly as I stared at the ghostly image of my dead boyfriend. With the sun rising higher in the sky to fill the world with light once more, I thought maybe, just maybe, he was right.

Maybe everything would be okay.

That's when I heard the front door crash open.

"Astra Arden!" An angry, commanding voice filled with fury pierced through the peaceful silence like a thunderbolt. "Astra Arden, you come out here and you face me!"

I raised an eyebrow. "Your mother?"

Jason nodded. "I said eventually things will be okay. I didn't say it would all work out today."

Oh, boy.

* * *

THANK YOU FOR READING!

I hope you enjoyed Owl in Due Curse. Please think about leaving a review! Astra, Archie and the whole Arden family continue their adventures in Book 11, Owl in Due Curse.

KEEP UP WITH LEANNE LEEDS

Thanks so much for reading! I hope you liked it! Want to keep up with me?

Visit leanneleeds.com to:

Find all my books…

Sign up for my newsletter…

Like me on Facebook…

Follow me on Twitter…

Follow me on Instagram…

Thanks again for reading!

Leanne Leeds

FIND A TYPO? LET US KNOW!

Typos happen. It's sad, but true.

Though we go over the manuscript multiple times, have editors, have beta readers, and advance readers it's inevitable that determined typos and mistakes sometimes find their way into a published book.

Did you find one? If you did, think about reporting it on leanneleeds.com so we can get it corrected.

Printed in Great Britain
by Amazon